SECRETS IN
SILVER

BOBBY BROWN

AUTHOR'S NOTE

Dear reader,

Welcome to my realm of imagination. Since my earliest days, I've been a devoted reader with a vivid imagination. My heart belongs to the genres of horror, mystery, and romance. As a child, I relished the adventures of leaping from one imaginary realm to another.

Beyond my passion for reading, I've discovered immense joy in crafting my fictional universes. The tales you'll find here were carefully woven for fellow mystery enthusiasts. I invite you to join me in a realm of secrets and suspense where you can lose yourself in thrilling stories.

Let's go!

Bobby Brown

SILVER

Silver is often regarded as a reflective hue, acting as a mirror to our inner selves, enabling us to perceive ourselves from an external perspective. It symbolizes strength, clarity, and concentration. Silver is associated with purity, signifying the journey towards self-purification, self-awareness, and recognizing both our strengths and areas for improvement.

The significance of the color silver extends to its potential influence. Silver is thought to enlighten the soul by removing obstacles within the body's energy pathways, thereby directing and harmonizing the body's energy flow. This luminous color is believed to serve as a guiding force on the path to spiritual enlightenment.

Silver is also associated with emotions, carrying a feminine energy that connects it to the moon and the rhythmic movement of tides. This hue is characterized by its fluidity, sensitivity, and an inherent air of mystery. Silver embodies a soothing and purifying essence, evoking calmness and tranquility.

When considering what the color silver reveals about one's personality, it often signifies an individual with a subtle yet pronounced sense of sophistication, dignity, and elegance. Those with a silver character are typically blessed with a blend of physical attractiveness, talent, and a charismatic demeanor, often seen as fortunate individuals. They exhibit grace, gentleness, and a non-confrontational nature while holding solid values and a moral compass.

THE FIRST SECRET

The caution tape only served to increase the curiosity of the crowd. It didn't help that the police cars, which formed a barrier around the entrance to the nightclub, were still flashing their red and blue lights, drawing partygoers off the main street like drunken moths to a rave.

Or whatever the phrase was.

Detective Selena Bellefontaine pushed through the crowd, bypassing a group of gawkers who reeked of sweetness and the unmistakable scent of tequila. She swiftly displayed her gleaming silver badge to the rookie responsible for crowd control, and he promptly raised the barrier tape to grant her access. On the other side of the tape, she could delve deeper into the investigation of the scene.

The ambulances had attempted to park strategically, forming a substantial physical barrier between the bystanders and the victims. Among those sheltered behind the barrier, most sat on the sidewalk, wrapped in space blankets, as paramedics attended to their needs. The soft glow of streetlamps provided gentle illumination for the scene. Judging by appearances, the injuries seemed relatively minor: young people dressed for a night of carousing, sporting smudged makeup, scraped knees, and vibrant beads dangling around their necks. The double doors were guarded by a beat cop, who appeared unharmed like the rest of the building. Selena didn't think the damage was too bad–until she stepped inside.

The Chandelier Club, aptly named for its overabundance of glittering chandeliers, resembled a scene where a stampede of enraged elephants had crashed through. Bits of crystals and pearls were shattered among chunks of drywall. The bar was transformed into a mosaic of broken glass, and the counter had been crushed in one place. Shards of wood stuck up from the counter, threatening to impale anyone careless enough to stumble onto it. Someone had flicked on the lights, yet traces of the fog machine's remnants lingered in the air, casting a hazy ambiance. Or maybe it was dust from the destruction.

The owner, probably, was talking animatedly with two detectives on the far side of the room. Forensics was still walking around taking pictures of the damage. The occasional bright flash from their cameras highlighted more of the chaotic scene. Selena was drawn to the dance floor, not by any passionate desire to dance but by the looming silhouette concealed beneath a white sheet. It leveled a height to her chest; she stood at five feet six inches in flats. It was hard to tell from the distorted shape what was concealed by the sheet, but the longer Selena stared, the more the ominous feeling grew in her mind. It was broader than the little bar tables shoved haphazardly to the room's perimeter.

"Must've been a helluva fight," Selena muttered to herself. She tucked her dark hair away and reached for the sheet.

"You might not want to look at that." Came a gruff but annoyingly familiar voice from behind.

Selena reluctantly turned. The detectives were finished talking to the owner and swaggered their way over to her. She turned away momentarily to hide her annoyed wince before turning to face them full-on.

"Detective, Thibodeaux." Selena acknowledged him wryly.

Roy Thibodeaux smoothed a pinky over his pencil-thin mustache. The contemptuous smirk, always hovering in the corner of his lips, broadened as he and his partner stopped in front of her. "Some real nastiness went on here tonight. And just when I thought I was gonna be stuck with the paperwork, we got a match on your perp's M.O."

Evans, Thibodeaux's usually silent lapdog, fanned some paperwork with a smarmy smile. Selena snatched them from him and examined the fresh Polaroids. She flipped through the handwritten paperwork until she found it. A tattoo, obscured by the smear of blood, appeared somewhere on the victim's upper arm.

Thibodeaux, who had been talking the entire time, tried to stop her when Selena pulled the sheet off the body. He and Evans recoiled. She nearly did too; the white sheet had been a blessing of forgiveness on the brutal decimation of the raw gore, but she wasted no time hurrying around to examine the body for herself. Twelve years on the New Orleans police force had strengthened her resolve and prepared her for anything.

The corpse was a man, maybe in his early thirties– it was hard to tell with his face's gruesome state. His clothing, torn shreds barely clung to the body, had turned almost pitch-black from the saturation of blood. His face, suspended in frozen horror, was turned up, and he was spread-eagled, almost on bended knees. Selena crouched down to get a closer look. It took her a moment to understand what she was looking at. It appeared he was speared by a mic stand that had been ripped off the stage.

"He's been shish kabobbed." Thibodeaux held a fist over his mouth in disgust. Evans made a halfhearted attempt at a laugh at his ill-timed joke. Selena glanced over her shoulder at him in veiled contempt.

She stood and grabbed some gloves to touch the body. Selena carefully examined his right arm before rigor mortis set in, then abandoned it to check the other side. She found what she was looking for on the underside of this left bicep.

The techs had conducted an image search, but unfortunately, they couldn't find the matching tattoos shared by the previous and current victims. Selena leaned in to examine the tattoo. To her, it looked like a goat with a crown. It was hard to make out since the body was crusted with blood, but there was smaller detailing around the goat's face that seemed like letters, but she hadn't been able to place them yet. She couldn't make out the details on this body, but she could tell the tattoo was the same.

Two victims brutally killed may be a coincidence. Three victims were a pattern. Selena's body stiffened as her blood ran cold, and she silently admitted a serial killer was out there, just in time for Mardi Gras.

"I see what you're thinking, Bellefontaine." Selena rolled her eyes over to Thibodeaux. Part of her wanted to forget he was there.

"Don't you have something else to do, Thibodeaux? This is my case now." Selena swiftly headed for the door, but he followed closely with determined steps.

"Yeah, you want it, you got it, but if the Chief hears you even whisper about this being a pattern, you'll be writing tickets for the meters until ya dead. Look..." He stopped her with a hand on the shoulder. She turned towards him, stoned face, and was mildly disappointed when he quickly raised his hands in surrender. She would have used any reason to strike him. "The media'll have a field day and use the Chief's ass as a frisbee if they hear there's a Mardi Gras killer. Once the holidays are over, we can deal with it then."

"Mardi Gras doesn't end for another, what, ten days? Who knows how many victims there'll be by then?" Thibodeaux shrugged, and Selena remembered precisely why she disliked him and all the other corrupt cops in her precinct. They cared more about financial gain and image rather than the victims.

Selena stormed out the back door to avoid the press, and Thibodeaux didn't try to stop her this time. "It's your funeral." He called after her, but she ignored him. She had work to do.

***

As the sun began to rise, Selena closed the door to her apartment with a kick. Ajan raced to greet her and twined around her ankles like a silky silver ribbon.

"I've got you, girl. Just let me get to the dish." Navigating the field of discarded clothes and her usual clutter, Selena carefully placed her box of files on the coffee table. Then, she made her way to the cabinet containing the cat food and opened it. Ajan tried to stick her face in the bag when she opened the closure, but Selena was wise to her tricks and held her back long enough to scoop some into her dish. Selena refreshed the water dish while Ajan devoured the food. Watching her cat with an amused but tired smile, Selena thought she ate like a dog, as Ajan nearly tipped over her bowl while she ate with wild abandon.

Selena put down the water bowl and poured a glass for herself. She stared out the kitchen window as she drank, watching the golden shimmer of the rising sun on the Mississippi River, hypnotized and exhausted.

She spent the entire night at the precinct, urging the police technicians to complete as many tests as possible. She snuck out before the Chief's early morning shift. It would take longer for the blood work to return, but Selena doubted it would show any other clues to link the cases. The last two victims were killed in unrelated locations. There was no known connection between them—except the tattoo, and they had been stabbed through the heart.

What disturbed her most about the cases, like the other crime scenes, was that there were no witnesses. Amidst the packed nightclub, bursting at the seams due to the Mardi Gras festivities and partygoers encircling the victim, no one could identify Paolo Savoie's assailant – the third victim of this mysterious killing spree. There had been a fight, that was for sure; the partiers mentioned a commotion of some kind, but no one saw who started it. Thankfully, but oddly, no one else was killed. The victim was targeted. Not even the witnesses closest to Savoie could identify the perp when he died in a crowded nightclub. Thankfully, the owner had preserved surveillance tapes that the forensics team would analyze - later.

Selena placed her empty glass in the sink and returned to the living room. She cleared off the couch enough that she had space to sit and found the remote wedged between the cushions. The owner still used old-fashioned VHS tapes in his security system. Perhaps, just the minimum to fulfill security protocols, as the low-quality footage wouldn't adequately capture the debauchery that unfolded within his establishment. Fortunately, Selena kept an old dual VHS/DVD player for this reason. She checked that the tape was rewound and popped it in. She would be careful to sneak it back to the evidence room.

The audio was garbled, and the footage was black and white. Selena sighed and rolled her eyes. Policing became increasingly challenging when individuals attempted to thwart law efforts. The owner must've been required to keep records for his insurance but didn't want to get the dealers who helped make his club so popular and recognizable. Selena got off the couch and sat on the edge of the coffee table. She squinted to try and make out the hazy figures.

The only camera was pointed mainly at the cash register and the bar, but the dance floor was barely visible behind it. The mass of dancers on the floor melded into an unrecognizable sea of undulating bodies. Just when Selena was sure that the tapes wouldn't be helpful, a commotion broke out from the right of the screen.

The dance floor blob quickly broke apart, and Selena was confident that at least one of the figures at the center of the chaos was the victim. She scooted closer to the television, her hazel eyes fixated on the screen. A flash of darkness interrupted the tape, and an odd roar that made her hair stand on end crackled from the speakers.

The darkness lasted only a few seconds before the

video feed returned, revealing a scene that had descended into utter chaos. People were running for the exits, and in less than five minutes, the club had cleared enough to see the destruction and the victim – dead. Just as Selena had found him when she arrived on the scene hours later. It had all happened in a matter of seconds. She took a moment to process the information and pet Ajan, who carved out a spot on her lap.

Selena had spent the entire night waiting for the tech experts to authenticate the tapes and had confirmed their authenticity. But the most crucial scene of all was missing from the footage. Not believing her eyes, she rewound the tape and watched the scuffle again. Savoie, she was sure it was him now, staggered back onto the floor, where she nearly lost sight of him. Then the tape went dark, and he was dead. She had to watch it ten more times to be sure, but she could keep an eye on him once she knew what she was looking for. One moment, he was standing there; the next, he was dead, and the most crucial scene was a black screen.

Selena got up to pace furiously, trying to decide where to place her rage. The owner could be lying, but how could he have had time to cut the tape well enough to hide it from the techies? The record showed that the first officers arrived fifteen minutes after the victim died.

The techies were an easy mark for her anger. Obviously, the tape had been altered. How? Did someone just kill the lights at the exact moment the victim was killed?

Selena's head started to throb with the first sign of a migraine. She hadn't expected to get stonewalled this quickly. The last two victims were all killed at night, during their regular routines in isolated places – no witnesses. She would let herself get her hopes up that surely, in the middle of a crowded dance club, someone had to have seen who had done it.

Selena hated to call it a night, but she had been up for 36 hours already. Her mind was clouded with anger, frustration, and curiosity. Some sleep would give her clarity to crack this case.

***

Selena awoke, startled by her blaring phone, and peeled her face off the pillow. It was the station. She ignored the call but leaped out of bed and rushed into a scalding shower. By the time she arrived at the station, she was clean in body, if not spirit.

The Chief leaned out of his office and barked her name before she even reached her desk. When she knocked perfunctorily on the door frame, he stood behind his desk, which was never a good sign. He only stood when he was spitting mad.

She noticed his white shirt was rumpled, and his thin tie was askew. His bushy mustache quivered as he gnawed on a cigar, trying to get his temper under control, looking at her with bloodshot, watery eyes. "Sit down, Bellefontaine." He snapped around the cigar.

She perched on one of the hard wooden chairs, leaving the door open. If the Chief were going to shout, everyone on the floor would be able to hear, and if he didn't shout, at least the cigar smoke would have somewhere to go.

"I want a progress report, detective. Where are you on this?" He pressed a meaty finger onto a stack of papers he had removed from her desk. He seemed calm, but Selena knew better and chose her words carefully.

"The latest victim has the same tattoo as the previous two. No other connections between them have been found so far." She started to give him the bare facts, but he cut her off.

"Have you ID'd the perp yet?" He snapped.

Selena gritted her teeth. "No, the tapes were inconclusive-"

"That's not good enough, detective!" He objected. His cheeks reddened with anger, but she beat him to it.

"I'm following the evidence, Chief!" She gritted out

with thinning tolerance for his blustering admonishment.

"This one was in public! Are you telling me you can't track one lead–" Spittle flew from his mouth, and his face turned a dangerous shade of red.

She bit out, "None of the witnesses saw anything, and the tapes–"

"I don't give a damn about the tapes! You need to get out there and–" Selena interrupted, her anger at the breaking point.

"And what? Bust some heads? Shake some trees? My guy's not going to be a coconut, Chief!" She snapped back, just shy of actually yelling at her boss.

He stared at her coldly, and she took a visual beating. The floor outside was eerily silent, so she knew everyone had heard her - not quite - yelling at the Chief. Selena did her best not to fidget or push her hair back in frustration like she wanted to. She refused to show weakness in an office of mostly men.

His voice was flat when he uttered the following statement. "If the media gets wind of this, the mayor will be all over me. I need results, Selena." She couldn't interpret the expression on his face, but it couldn't be good that he had resorted to using her first name. "So, you're getting a partner." He held up a hand when she leaped to her feet, and she knew from the look in his eye that she shouldn't push him on this right now, but she tried.

Her fingernails bit into her palms. "I don't need some rookie–"

His voice elevated. "You're not getting a rookie. You're getting an experienced detective–"

"If you pair me with Evans, I'll quit right now." She said in a low voice but slumped back into her chair.

"No, I'm not giving you Evans. Look, will you just shut up and let me finish already?" He sounded furious but sighed long and low when he dropped into the chair behind his desk. "He's from Boston and has a strong record. I think you'll…well, you'll probably hate him. I haven't seen you like anybody in the twelve years you've been working here, but you'll probably hate this guy less than other guys. He needed a partner anyway, and lucky for me, he volunteered to work with you." His chair squeaked as he leaned forward to shout, "Archer! Get in here!"

She heard footsteps in the doorway moments later but didn't rush to turn around. Selena stared at the ceiling momentarily to silently ask God what she had done to deserve this before turning in her chair to face her punishment.

Detective Archer joined their department about a month ago, but she hadn't paid him much attention. He had an air of arrogance that Selena did not care for. She looked closely at him now. He was younger than she expected. He looked fit, so she wouldn't have to worry about him dying of a heart attack during their first pursuit. The Chief introduced them as if they didn't already know each other. "Detective Brad Archer, this is your new partner, Detective Selena Bellefontaine."

Selena scrutinized him thoroughly, not bothering to hide her lack of enthusiasm. Archer, at least, had some manners and offered her a stiff hand while searching her face before he piped up. "Hello, detective. It's a pleasure to meet you. I was with the Boston force for more than ten years, so I won't slow you down." His charming smile didn't quite seem to reach his dark brown eyes, but it was welcoming without being cloying. In another life, Selena might've thought he was a handsome guy.

She stood, turning her focus back to the Chief. Selena leaned over the desk, palms flat on the surface, just close enough that the cigar smell didn't knock her out. "I. Don't. Need. Help." She gritted out, not bothering to hide her contempt from 'Archer.'

"Have you got any leads?" The Chief met her stare, unimpressed.

Selena hesitated, unwilling to go down without a fight. She may not yet have a clear lead, but she wasn't out of options yet. "Give me 24 hours." She pleaded.

"Can't do that. The first victim died on the first day of Mardi Gras, four days ago. Three bodies in four days! At this rate, we might be up to our ears before the week is over." He kept his voice low, not wanting to be overheard. He leaned back in his chair, and Selena knew she had lost this one.

She sighed with the pain of exasperation. Great. Now, she would need to solve this case while towing extra baggage.

Archer followed her into the hall and to her desk. It wasn't until he sat at the desk across from hers that she paid him any attention. She scanned the desk in front of her mournfully. He had already started cleaning up the piles of her paperwork that spilled over from her desk, uncovering the outdated calendar from two years ago. Selena scowled.

Her desk was a bit messier now as she recollected old files and stacked them until they tilted like the Leaning Tower of Pisa, towering onto one another for support. He leaned back in his chair, watching her with keen interest. She felt her scowl deepen.

"Look, Brad."

He winced, but his lingering smile wasn't deterred. "Can I at least get 'detective'?" He sat up, meeting her eyes when she glared at him. "I'm not asking you to be my new best friend or trust me right away." Something about him surprised Selena, and just now, she realized what it was – she hadn't seen a cop with such an open, playful look in his eye since she left the academy. "But I've solved murders, been shot at, and even cracked a cold case or two. I promise I won't get in your way, and I'll do whatever I can to be helpful to you on this case." His smile widened, turning that 'winning charm' of his back on. "What'd you say? Can we start on a…last-name basis?"

She leaned forward, letting herself smile back. "Sure, Detective Archer." He had been with the precinct for approximately a month, and she rarely interacted with him. She wasn't about to start now. "I've got some evidence to go through." She patted the pile next to her. "Why don't you get us some coffee, and we'll start on it together?"

Archer's smile widened, showing off his perfect teeth. "Sure thing, boss." While he got to and went to the break room, Selena grabbed her bag and headed out the door.

***

The sun was beating down mercilessly on the French Quarter. Some years, Mardi Gras was chilly. Maybe not surprising for early March, but this year was unseasonably warm. She took a streetcar from mid-city down into the Quarter, not wanting her new shadow to follow her too quickly. She had to see a man about the tape but had to maneuver through the crowded streets filled with drunks and scantily clad women.

Jimmy was a bit squirrely, but she had helped him out of a jam a few years back, and sometimes, if the motivation was right, he helped her when she wasn't sure she could trust the techies. The precinct was almost a second home to her; that's how she knew that sometimes, inconvenient truths would go missing, usually in the basement where they did the testing.

She found Jimmy in his usual place, selling trinkets and knockoffs to tourists, crammed into a tiny shop in what could accurately be described as an alleyway. She eyed the new bullet holes in the sign that read "French Quarter Corner" and wondered how long after the last time she had been there those had been installed.

The door opened with a cheery little chime. The tiny shop was crowded with clean shelves, from key chains to plastic shrunken heads to Mardi Gras beads. The walls, where they were visible, were covered in signs.

Most were novelty signs with famous street names. Selena knew the actual merchandise was not displayed on the shelves.

Jimmy bustled out of the back and greeted warmly. "Welcome to the French Qu-" The smile dropped when he recognized her and bustled over to her quickly, glancing around the empty shop. "What're ya doin' here, Selena?" He dared not call her detective in case the walls were listening. "This is a bad time." He gently pushed on her shoulder as if that would get her to budge, but she planted her feet.

"I'm here on business, Jimmy." She tilted her head to the back room where he emerged. She wanted to ask what had him so spooked, but if she pushed too hard, he might clam up. Besides, he was probably more into something he shouldn't be, but with Jimmy, it was usually small-time stuff. "I just need you to verify a tape, and I'm outta your hair."

He tilted his head and looked down from his tall, wiry body as he eyed her thoughtfully. His taut midriff peeped out from under his tight crop top. Jimmy was smart as a whip and more cautious than a retired cop. He hesitated for a moment, and she waited, letting him think it over. "Yeah? Just check it and make sure it's legit?" He smoothed a hand over his forehead to wipe away the sweat.

"That's the one." Selena gently pulled the tape from her bag, presenting it as if offering a morsel to a young bird. "Check it out; let me know what you find." She implored in a sweet voice.

Jimmy casually studied the tape, turning it over in his hands. Not knowing it held the key to unlocking Selena's case. "Okay. Okay, for you, Selena."

She snagged a candy from the counter display and slapped fifty dollars on the counter, which Jimmy snapped up. "Thanks, Jimmy."

"I'll call you when I'm done." She let him rush her out, back into the heat. Selena twirled her dark brown hair into a high ponytail and let it hang down her shoulders. She walked along the street, in no hurry to return to the station. The main streets were starting to get more crowded. Most partiers were still in bed, but the tourists were too ubiquitous to be absent from the roads for long.

Selena followed the cooling breeze from the river while eating breakfast. The chocolate croissant was starting to melt, but she savored it as much as possible. As she thought about stopping for real food, something flashed brightly and caught her eye in a store window. It seemed to signal her with short bursts of silver light. She halted with stark curiosity and moved closer to the window to escape the tight flow of the foot traffic. There were fewer people here, mostly dressed in ludicrous costumes, and she ignored them while she scanned the display for whatever it was that had caught her attention.

It was an antique store, according to the painted sign above the window and the worn items trying their best to remain proudly on display. There were dolls with porcelain faces sitting in their tiny Victorian chairs. Insidious smiles plastered on their little faces as if teasing Selena that they knew a secret she didn't. Beaded pillows, old appliances, and birdhouses, among other knickknacks. Selena scanned each item and gave up when her eyes fell on the smaller objects near the front. There were several pieces of jewelry. The owner of the shop hadn't quite wanted to polish away all the tarnish on the silver (since it wouldn't look antique if they shined), but when she turned her head and shifted a bit from side to side, she caught a glimpse of a familiar etching on a silver locket.

Selena had to lean until her face was nearly touching the glass to be sure, but as soon as she was, she stormed into the shop. The shop was quiet and blessedly calm, and Selena wasted no time finding the counter.

She rang the bell insistently, constraining herself

just enough to try not to piss off whomever the bell would summon. A primly dressed middle-aged woman appeared from the beaded drapery behind the counter and touched the bell gently to stop the reverberating 'ding.' When it was quiet, she asked, "How can I help you?"

"I'd like to see the silver locket with the goat in the window," Selena asked as calmly as she could. The shopkeeper's smile softened with commercial pleasure.

"One moment, please." She left to the window, and Selena kept an eye on her without following her to the window – she didn't want to draw attention to it. Yet.

"Here we are." She laid the locket on a black velvet pad on the countertop, reminiscent of an upscale jewelry store. Selena picked it up and held it under the lamp to examine it closely. Sure enough, there was no mistaking it: the strange, crowned goat tattoo shared by all the victims was also lightly embossed on the surface of the locket.

Instead of the cold surface she expected from a silver locket, it was surprisingly warm in her hands. Selena looked back at the shopkeeper and put on her best smile. The woman looked at her suspiciously, and Selena toned it down a bit. "Can you tell me anything about this locket?"

"It's an antique, of course. I don't have a certificate

of authenticity." Her sugary tone never wavered. "But it's early 1700s by the craftsman's mark." She indicated a tiny trademark on the inside Selena would have overlooked.

"Where did you get it?" Selena's question was too abrupt. She could tell by the surprised hesitation in the other woman's demeanor.

"People constantly bring in items. If you're worried about quality, we have an appraiser who can verify that it's silver."

Selena slowed her pace and intentionally softened her stance. "That's alright. I was merely intrigued by the image. It doesn't quite capture its beauty."

But the store owner wanted to capture a sale. "It will be more beautiful once I polish it up."

Selena was afraid essential details would be removed or altered. "That's okay, I'll take it as is."

"So, you'd be interested in buying it?" The shopkeeper's smile added a few teeth.

"Yes." Selena tried to keep the strain out of her tone. The shopkeeper began punching buttons on a calculator to show her the price. Selena tried not to balk at the final price. Selena wasn't interested in haggling. She was only interested in purchasing the mysterious locket. "Do you keep any record from the previous owners?"

The woman shot her a sharp look, but Selena had

her warmest smile and widened her eyes, aiming for naïveté. It must've worked since the woman relaxed again. "We keep records for purchases but not for distribution. Our patron's privacy is paramount." She rested a protective hand on the black filing cabinet mostly obscured behind the counter.

Selena noted the movement but didn't follow it with her eyes. "Of course." She finished ringing Selena up. Selena left the shop with more questions and fewer answers than she had hoped.

She found a semi-secluded bench to examine the necklace. The shopkeeper had been surprisingly skittish, and Selena didn't want to push her too hard until she knew what she was looking for.

A tattoo shared by three strangers with no connections and an ancient locket she stumbled upon in an antique shop. It was an unexpected break, but Selena didn't know what it meant.

The locket may have been rusted shut. The clasp didn't pop open as it should have. She turned the locket over and noticed an engraving on the back: "*Vers le Haut, Seigneur Taureau.*" She couldn't translate it and sighed loudly with exasperation, catching looks from the passersby. She looked at it again. It looked like it was written in French or maybe Latin. She pulled her phone from her pocket, but it was dead. Selena rubbed her temple and reminded herself to be patient. She was just getting started.

✻✻✻

Selena decided not to mention the locket to Archer when she returned to the station. She kept it stowed in the pocket of her jeans. When the elevator doors slid open, pandemonium burst forth. She readied her stance before she saw that everything was under control.

A procession of crimson, sonorously angry, and odorously drunk tourists were paraded toward booking. They would probably be held overnight until they cooled off – fights during Mardi Gras weren't uncommon, though they had been on an upswing lately. She held the door until the crowd dispersed enough for her to exit the elevator and returned to her desk.

Archer was examining something on his lap, apparently working, as she approached. A cold cup of coffee waited for her beside the stack of papers. Surprisingly, her new partner didn't look up when she sat down. She almost laughed. Was he giving her the silent treatment?

He fidgeted, and she lifted the cold cup to her mouth to hide her smirk and took a cautious sip. "Thanks for the coffee." He stiffly looked up then, aiming for nonchalance and overshooting the mark.

"Glad you like it." He said tautly but couldn't resist going a little further. "Back already?"

"Just beating some trees." She said, sitting back in her chair and no longer bothering to hide her smirk. "Find anything while I was gone?"

"Actually, yes." He said in a tone that was just huffy enough that Selena almost 'awwed' at how cute it was. He tossed a yearbook down on the desk in front of her and set another on top so she could still see the left page of the lower book. She recognized them before he walked around to touch the faces.

She bolted upright in her chair and examined the third book he placed in front of her. The faces and their dated haircuts, albeit dated, were those of the victims. Selena snatched the books and studied them further. Each was from different years, given the difference in the victim's ages.

"They all went to the same school?" Selena flipped the books over. "Castille Preparatory School," she noted to herself. Selena had briefly heard of it. It was a private school just outside the city limits. How was he able to connect the dots so quickly?

"They all participated in the same club." She tossed

an annoyed glance at his growing smirk.

Selena didn't acknowledge his answer and checked for herself. She tossed the books aside and reached for her phone. Archer plucked the phone from her hand, and she shot him a disapproving look.

"I already made an appointment for us." Selena quickly went from annoyance (how could he make contact without her) to eagerness – they had a solid lead!

"When is it?" Selena plugged in her phone.

"Can I come this time?" She ignored his sarcastic question, but he grabbed his key, scrutinizing her face with an arrogant smile. She tried not to hold it against him. It was his lead, never mind how irritating it was that he had found it so quickly. She reminded herself that he wasn't new to the force - they also had crimes in Boston.

She wanted to say no very badly, but the word died on her tongue. "Fine." She grumbled. "When?"

"The vice principal is expecting us in an hour." Archer all but bounced on his heels.

Selena didn't wait. She grabbed her phone and marched towards the elevator, leaving Archer to catch up. He slid into the elevator beside her before the doors closed. "You shouldn't have contacted the school without talking to me first."

"I would have contacted you first if you'd told me

where you were going or when you'd be back." He was pouting again, but maybe that was partly her fault. The more she thought about it, the more she cooled off. She probably would have done the same thing if she had broken the lead herself. He kept to the far end of the elevator and asked what she considered an odd question. "You seem different. Did something happen while you were out?"

She frowned at him. Her detective's brain asked how he could have detected something different when he didn't know her. She didn't know how to answer the question. "I put my hair in a ponytail."

She opted for a police car. It promised the quickest escape from the city. While they didn't have designated vehicles reserved exclusively for their use, the detectives had the privilege of selecting any available car, so he grabbed one of the discreet vehicles with concealed lights and sirens. The GPS said they would arrive in forty-five minutes, but she didn't mind being early. She preferred it.

Letting Archer drive also allowed her to research the school. None of the victims had attended the school simultaneously, yet somehow, they were all members of the French club. She made a mental note to investigate that odd little detail further. It would have been so tidy if they were all part of the same class, but they weren't. The first and third victims were closest in age, but they were still seven years apart – no way would they have attended the school at the same time, and she couldn't find evidence that they had ever met. It meant that even if this were the missing connection between the victims, the pool of potential targets would be everyone who had been part of the French club at Castille Prep every year. Too many potential victims, there had to be hundreds –.

"Bellefontaine." Archer waved a hand in front of her face. She peered up from her phone to realize they were parked in the closest available spot in front of the school. She had been so lost in thought she hadn't noticed.

Selena wasted no time throwing open her door and striding towards the school. Archer reached her just before she hit the sidewalk and pressed the button to lock the car, causing it to honk. She rolled her eyes again. How meticulous of him.

"Were you listening before?" He pressed. "I was saying there was a reason I asked to meet with the vice principal."

"Oh, yeah?" Selena tried to sound interested, pretending she hadn't utterly ignored him on the ride. She couldn't help it; this was too good a lead, and her mind was abuzz with dissecting the new possibilities.

Archer extended a hand in front of her, and she stopped. She turned to scrutinize him instead of bouncing up and down with excitement. "This guy, his name's Vincent La Bauve. He's been the French club teacher for the last twenty years before he was promoted to vice president." He leaned slightly towards her, his eyes alight with eagerness. "I think we've got our guy." He uttered in a low voice, soft but loaded with intrigue.

Selena scoffed. "Maybe. We'll see." She couldn't wait and surged into the school's reception area. The kindly older woman behind the desk greeted them warmly, but her perfectly coiffed bun and fierce eyes showed she wouldn't put up with any nonsense.

"Welcome. Are you here to see Mr. La Bauve?" They nodded in response, simultaneously producing their identification. With a polite smile, the receptionist nodded at their silver badges and vanished into the inner sanctum of a side office. Selena performed a sweeping glance at the large room with oversized windows. Pictures of graduating classes lined the walls and the obligatory case of school trophies. It was definitely a better school than the ones she had attended, that was certain. Being bounced around the foster care system gave her a good sample size. The kids who went here must have had wealthy parents. They likely resided on the expansive properties surrounding this neighborhood, hidden from view to keep their grand mansions concealed.

"Detectives." A robust man with speckled gray hair appeared with the receptionist, who dutifully went back to her desk. "Detectives, we can talk in my office." He regarded Archer under thick eyelashes before gesturing for them to enter with a sweeping motion of his hands.

While they followed him back to his office, Selena replayed his accent in her head, trying to place it. It sounded French, but having lived in New Orleans all her life, she recognized a hint of Cajun.

His office was large and tidy, with a panoramic view of the landscaping visible through the window behind his desk. "Now." He said, his stout body sitting stiffly behind his desk. "How can I help you?"

Selena sat in the chair opposite, but Archer hung back, eyeing the certifications and pictures on the walls. Selena took points. "Hello, sir. I'm Detective Selena Bellefontaine. We wanted to talk to you about some former students of yours."

Selena pulled the most recent pictures of the victims from the case file and presented them to the vice principal, who took them with a hand that trembled slightly.

"Excuse me, I have to go to the bathroom." Archer walked away before Selena waved a dismissive hand.

"Do you recognize them?" She asked pensively, already knowing the answer.

He hesitated for a long time, and she prepared herself for a lie, but he surprised her with a low, "Yes, though I haven't seen them for several years now. I understand they were killed recently."

Selena tried to hide her surprise. "Yes." She noted the sweat beading on his forehead and the slight flutter of his hands as if he didn't know what to do with them. "I'm surprised you didn't come forward with information if you knew the victims."

"Like I said, I haven't seen them in years. I didn't think there was any useful information I could give." He pushed his chair back and glanced covertly at her. He leaned forward again and studied her face. "Have you always lived in New Orleans? Detective…Breaux, did you say?"

"It's Bellefontaine." She corrected. "And yes."

"I'm sorry. It's just that you resemble a former student." Selena watched him suspiciously as he reached a filing cabinet tucked discreetly in a corner. He turned back after only a moment of rifling through it, this time with a class picture. He sat in his chair and held the picture, pointing to a face in the middle of the back row. Selena leaned in indulgently. The face was hard to make out – the date at the bottom said it was from over twenty years ago, so the camera that captured the moment and the picture itself were both faded.

Selena took the picture from him to inspect it closely. The face was oddly familiar, but she couldn't be sure. The young woman in the picture was probably in her late teens when the photo was taken. Her dark hair fell around her shoulders, and her smile was genuine. Selena's gaze settled on a subtle shimmer around her neck, which appeared to be a locket. It was nearly invisible, but the camera caught a fleeting sparkle of silver. "I wish I had a better picture of her." He intruded on her concentrated efforts to verify the locket. "Do you recognize her?" Selena glanced at him since his tone was odd, and he was leaning forward with anticipation in his chair, watching her with an intentness that made her uncomfortable enough to turn the picture face down on his desk. This was not her focus right now.

"No. Why?" She said, trying to keep impatience out of her tone.

"Her name was Delphine LeBlanc, and she later married Breaux. She was one of my brightest students." He sighed and leaned back in his chair. His tone changed, and became almost wistful.

After a pause, Selena broke the silence. "Was she also in the French club then?"

He gave a nervous chuckle that shook his chest without sound. "Yes. Yes, she was quite good at the French club." He said, stressing the last words slightly. "Are you sure there's nothing familiar about her that you recognize?"

On impulse, Selena pulled the locket from her pocket and let it hang over the back of her knuckles so he could see it. His reaction was immediate; he looked from the locket to her with stunned intensity.

Selena was getting itchy and wanted to cut to the chase. She asked bluntly, searching his eyes, "Sir, can you think of any reason or person who may be targeting your former students?" He stared at her, and Selena could see it in his eyes. He knew the answer. It was hovering between them, unspoken, while he studied her face, looking for...something.

He stood suddenly, and she stood with him. He came around the desk and seized her hands in his, imploring. "You'll need to be careful." He said in a harsh whisper, and his blue eyes said more than he could verbally communicate. "This is especially dangerous for you."

"Did I miss anything?" Archer stood in the doorway with his hand raised in a halfhearted impression of a knock. He had his usual casual air but glanced suspiciously at La Bauve's hands on hers.

Selena pulled away and hastily gathered her files, discreetly tucking the locket out of sight and letting her hair fall in front of her face to mask her reaction. La Bauve scooped up the photo he had shown her and pushed it between her files. Their eyes locked for a moment, and she understood the silent hint. Her body tensed with an unnerving thought that she was close to finding the missing piece of the puzzle. Could the clue lie in the photo he gave her? Her mind was reeling, trying to put everything into place.

"Thank you for your time," Selena muttered goodbye and left, walking past Archer, who lingered in the doorway.

She kept glancing at Archer on their way back to the car. He didn't mention what happened in the office but must've seen it. He must have had questions. How long had he been standing there anyway? Wasn't he curious why the vice principal was holding her hand?

She prepared herself for that question when he turned to look at her. Instead, he asked with a thin smile, "Are you hungry? I'm *starving*."

They stopped for some typical southern cuisine on the way back, but it wasn't until they were back in the car on their way to the station again that Archer said anything about the case. "So? The vice principal seemed nervous, right?"

"Yeah." She said reflexively, but her mind was tugging on another thread now.

"Are you convinced he did it?" Archer continued.

"No, he doesn't strike me as that type," she mused, trying to stay focused on her thread of thought. "How long have you been living in New Orleans?"

She caught him off guard since he grimaced and glanced at her repetitively. "Why? I recently moved here from Boston, remember?" He confirmed as if trying to convince himself. Yet, she couldn't ignore how he ordered food with the ease of a New Orleans native, but she tucked that thought away.

"Yeah. I was just asking since a lot of out-of-towners don't know about New Orleans' history of secret societies." She was looking out the window, watching the brightly colored Riverfront streetcar roll by and her thoughts getting lost in the shuffle of tourists.

Archer hesitated, then burst into laughter - a surprised, almost disbelieving outburst. "What? Seriously?"

"Mardi Gras evolved from one actually." She informed the window; her mind was gnawing at something just beyond its grasp.

She forgot about Archer for a minute until he spoke suddenly. "So, you think this guy is running a secret Société, and now he's killing off former members during Mardi Gras?" He said it with the enthusiasm of someone who had just discovered the coolest thing ever. She glanced at him, and he wore a smile reminiscent of a kid in a theme park. "You're as smart as they say you are. I hope this case turns out to be that cool."

She huffed a laugh and turned away when he smiled wider at her; he was delighted she had relented in her outward disdain for him, even if it was only a *tiny* bit. She shrugged, not wanting to reveal more. She wasn't sure how much she could trust this stranger. "Maybe." She glanced sideways at him. Deep thoughts were buried under his lake-green eyes. He cast his eyes straight ahead. "Vice Principal La Bauve knows something. That's for sure."

Archer didn't have anything to say to that, so they rode back to the station in silence. It was almost sunset by the time they pulled up, so they said goodbye for the evening and went their separate ways.

Archer wasn't as bad as she had initially feared, but

there was something she needed to do tonight, and she couldn't tell him for several reasons. One, she didn't want him tagging along. Two, she didn't know what she was searching for. And three, even if she did know him, she didn't fully trust anyone after her partner Aimee was murdered two years ago.

∗∗∗

Selena pulled up as close to the Castille Preparatory School as she dared without risking being spotted. When Archer drove the previous day, she had missed the massive iron gates to the entrance of the property. The rest of the journey would have to be on foot. On the drive back, she noticed several meandering streams around Castille Preparatory, and some old oak trees spotted the grounds. They were as much cover as she would get on her approach.

She fingered the almost smooth engraving of the locket in her pocket. She had a feeling, a strong surge of intuition, that there was more to be learned at Castille Prep. Selena planned to see what she could find after hours, especially in Vice Principal La Bauve's office. She had no justification for a warrant, so this would be solely off the record, but it had to be done to make progress on the case. Selena sighed heavily, fearing she may be on the cusp of crookedness by silently justifying this illegal search. Secret societies kept all kinds of things hidden, but her best lead was still the vice principal and his discreet filing cabinet.

Selena had to double back several times when she spotted a patrolling security guard or almost triggered a floodlight. "For a school, they've got a lot of damn security." She muttered to herself after the fifth time she was forced back. A small pier on a nearby lake caught her eye, and she got a clever idea.

The ride on the lake in the small rowing boat was neither comfortable nor swift, but it allowed her to avoid the patrol and floodlights. The school designer had never envisioned someone approaching by an abandoned rowboat traveling at a snail's pace. Downside: she had to keep lifting her head to check her position along the lake. Another downside: she didn't have a plan for getting to shore. She was doing her best to lie flat in the tiny boat, and her extended arms started to get a cramp. The campus itself was unreasonably pitch black. Which she thought was odd. Most schools were lit at night for security reasons, and the interior of this school was ominously dark. Not even a security light or an overachieving faculty member staying late had left a single light on in the building.

She finally found an upside. The school possessed a private dock nestled beneath an ancient wooden shelter permeated with the scent of swamp water and old money. Selena managed to sit up and lean out of the boat to grasp the side of the covered dock as it approached, gently nudging aside other boats that seemed to belong to their row team. The boat she was in was small enough that she was able to pull herself into the sheltering shadows. She pulled the boat onto the pier so it wouldn't drift away.

When she snuck out from under the covered dock, there was only a short gap between her and one of the side entrances to the main building, and she reached it without trouble. The door wasn't locked, and the interior of the building yawned open in front of her. The hair on the back of her neck stood up, and she hesitated with the handle partly turned.

Illegal fireworks from the Mardi Gras parade near the Mississippi River bathed the building's exterior and her skin in a vivid green hue. Yet, the area beyond the doorway remained as obscured as a pitch-black abyss that tried to scare her away with the implicit threat of the unknown. Selena never liked threats. Driven by a strong sense of curiosity, she mustered the strength to step inside. There was a reason the vice principal gave her that photo. Had that student been wearing a similar locket? Why was someone targeting former members of a high school French Club? And why did he warn her to be careful? She was neither a former student of the school nor a member of any French club.

The door closed behind her with muted finality. Selena stood frozen for a long moment; the dark was so deep it felt like a blanket pressed against her face. Slowly, her eyes adjusted to the darkness so subtly she thought she might be imagining it. Ahead, she perceived a vague light and instinctively stepped towards it. Her heartbeat was a constant staccato, rising and falling with her fear, but her footsteps echoed loudly to her ears, profaning the perfect seclusion of the darkness.

Shapes loomed around her as uneven shadows and glittering mirages. In her mind's eye, she knew they were just trophy cases or lockers and whatever other things schools had in their hallways. But at this moment, it was difficult to shake the feeling that she had entered an entirely different world. Something was disturbing on a primal level about this kind of darkness.

A faint light took her around a corner, and she continued to follow it. The barest light seemed, at times, to brighten, but she couldn't be sure of that either. Her only choice was to move forward.

An unfamiliar sound halted her progress abruptly.

She concentrated, trying to silence the thunderous beating of her heart while straining her senses to detect the source of the noise. It echoed in an empty and unending manner, like an eternal inhalation without a subsequent exhalation. Its constant pull and descent sent shivers down her spine, a sensation even more unsettling than any other she had encountered. A frigid breath brushed against her neck, causing the sweat to turn cold. She refused to remain motionless, as it left her feeling vulnerable. Advancing seemed like the only option; it would, at least, lead her to some tangible presence, whether for better or for worse.

A faint murmur accompanied by a flickering light from around the next corner caused Selena to halt once more. This time, it was unmistakable. As she approached, she discerned the elongated shadows of a doorway cast by an uncertain light. The dim illumination seeped through a narrow opening in a door situated at the far end of the corridor. The shifting, irregular light played tricks on the reflective floor, causing the shadows to dance in unpredictable patterns. The sound echoed again, growing louder and more distinct with each repetition. It was undoubtedly a human voice, signaling that someone else was present in the vicinity. However, Selena remained too distant to decipher the words, which reverberated and darted through the cavernous hallways.

She picked up her pace, moving faster and faster as the voice grew louder. She still couldn't understand it, but the voice was sharp with anger. A second shrill voice joined the first, making the noise more incomprehensible. As Selena sprinted through the shadowy corridors, the cacophonous thrumming grew louder, reverberating through the darkness. The voice that followed was a chilling symphony of her darkest memories and nightmares, emerging from the abyss of her heart. Her body moved on pure instinct, propelling her forward as a relentless wave of her deepest fears crashed down upon her.

And then they were gone.

Selena stopped abruptly, her rubber sole boots squeaking on the polished concrete floor. She found herself standing in the receptionist area of the school. The vast area was vaguely illuminated by the wall of windows across from her that allowed the soft glow of the moonlight to seep in from the outside.

Her attention wasn't on the muted room. Instead, her eyes were drawn to the only color, the expanding pool of red around the body of Vice Principal La Bauve.

Selena stared for a moment, her shock

immobilizing her as she gradually descended from her abject terror. A sudden, shadowy figure jolted her mind into alertness, and she directed her gaze toward the obscure silhouette emerging from the hidden corner of the room.

The outline of the clothed figure appeared in human form, as far as she could make out in the dark. As it drew closer to Selena, she noticed a purple masquerade mask further obscured the face, and the body was shrouded in a black hooded robe. The only movement Selena could muster was to blink in her frozen stance, trying to bring the dark figure into focus or into her reality. It can't be real. She tried to convince herself, even as it – glided and hovered in front of her. The black robe concealed all of the body, but a dark hand reached for her neck. "Wait," Selena choked in a shaky voice.

It suddenly stopped on her timid command. Only several feet from her, it tilted its dark head as if perplexed. The burst of fireworks flashed through the window, and Selena staggered backward, knocked over by an inconceivable thought. The masked figure had no face.

Several seconds later, she couldn't be sure of the accuracy of her eyes. The shrouded figure blended into the darkness and disappeared. "Stop!" She shouted in a much louder voice, but it had already disappeared. Her legs felt feeble, her body chilled and rigid.

Selena turned back to the body of Vice Principal La Bauve. She was about to retrieve the flashlight beside him but had second thoughts. She remembered not to touch anything at a crime scene with ungloved hands. She observed the dagger in his chest with an odd sense of loss.

Minutes passed before she had the presence of mind to report the crime. She waited for the medics and police to arrive in silence. She didn't need them to tell her that he had died of a stab wound to the heart. A single fatal blow buried the finger guard and partial handle. Selena had some time to figure out the brutality of the situation before the forensics team arrived. She had to quickly figure out how to explain her presence at the scene.

She had seen the killer, but she wouldn't be able to give any useful information on how to find him. So, she did the best she could. The detectives analyzed her suspiciously as she reported she had a hunch, and when she came in, she saw a hooded figure running away from the body.

That's all she could tell them, but Selena had a faint realization that she may have more details to work on. She might know exactly who he was!

Selena was not surprised that she was put on administrative leave for the events at Castille Preparatory School. The media was beside themselves that the beloved teacher and Vice Principal, Mr. La Bauve, was killed in such a brutal fashion in the middle of Mardi Gras.

So, of course, the incompetent detective in charge of the case was suspended for negligence, trespassing, etcetera, and so on. Selena nursed her coffee and mindlessly petted Ajan, who purred contentedly in her lap. The media hounded her day and night for interviews about her stunning incompetence. She only took one call from Jimmy, confirming that the tape she had brought him was authentic, just as the techs had said. After that, she let her phone die and ignored the regular knocks on her door while she planned her next move. At least she had time to clean her apartment.

Mystery and danger were a part of the lifeblood of New Orleans. Tourists came to sample that taste of debauchery and intrigue for a few weeks a year. Some believed they were attuned to the undercurrent of black magic and unexplainable phenomena. They weren't. At least not enough to break into the deep undercurrent of secrets as old as the city itself. But Selena didn't believe in black magic and unexplainable phenomena. There was an explanation for everything. She just needed time to figure it out.

When Selena was four years old, her mother entered her room one fateful night, her voice trembling with fear as she hurriedly hid Selena in the closet. Little did Selena know that as her mother left that room, it would be the last time she ever laid eyes on her.

They never found who killed her parents, but the unforgettable sounds she heard that night were repressed memories that occasionally surfaced during her nightmares. She heard those same sounds again that night at the prep school. Ethereal sounds that transcended the abilities of mere mortals. But detectives could not arrest a shrouded faceless figure. The pressure was on to give them something tangible – and quickly.

New Orleans possessed a unique beauty she believed was unmatched anywhere else in the world, but it also harbored a danger she hoped never to encounter. She had seen terrible and captivating things during her life in New Orleans, some of which seemed unexplainable to outsiders. But they were staged performances to enhance the mysterious lure of New Orleans. For those who called it home year-round, it was simply a part of everyday life. But those things would eventually be justified by the police department.

Selena had joined the police force after she aged out of the foster care system because she hoped there could be some redemption in her work. So that she could help people, find people, and bring some peace to those left behind. The corruption she had found instead almost broke her spirit. Then she remembered that fateful night when she had lost her family and home, and she had found the strength to persevere. In the darkest of times, is when light was needed the most.

Selena had waited a long time to make a difference, and she could feel that now was the moment she waited for. She waited what seemed like an eternity that night before slipping into the hallway, down a floor, and climbing out the window on the other side of the apartment building.

Her dark clothes and domino mask blended with the increasing crowds on the streets, and she quietly slipped past the indiscreet media trucks lurking outside her building waiting for her to emerge.

***

Sebastien Mouton was a well-known secret in New Orleans. He had been on the city council several times, partly because of his compassionate policies. She had always liked the small, distinctive scar on his chin. Selena thought it added character to his perfect looks, giving him the appearance of a man who engaged in unscrupulous activities for a living, despite hailing from a well-off family that resided in New Orleans since it was just a small port. Maybe even before that, or so the rumors said. She couldn't be a hundred percent certain; her limited funds didn't allow her to mingle with the upper crust, but she had a strong suspicion that she recognized the mask worn by the shrouded figure.

Secret societies had founded this city. In her opinion, they had been drawn to the opportunities, the riches, and the dark secrets native to the land. They mostly kept to themselves, concerned only with their internal matters, but once in a great while, their wars would spill onto the streets as one prominent family tried to amass power over the other. The killings were usually so brutal or arcane that people refused to discuss them openly—those who did often met with sudden tragic ends. Selena felt somewhat shielded behind her silver badge. It provided fragile protection that could be shattered if she was not careful where she trod.

Unlike some of the other heirs to wealthy families, Sebastien Mouton lived alone in the French Quarter. His parents passed away two years ago within months of each other. The newspaper printed that they died from natural causes, which puzzled Selena. They were a mature couple but didn't seem the elderly type to die of old age. Scandal surrounded their deaths, and Selena had escorted him back to his townhouse when he felt threatened by disapproving constituents. She still remembered its location. One of the items she remembered from his lavish townhouse was the purple mask. It stood out because it was encased in a glass box. He explained that it had been in his family for generations. It was imported from Venice, Italy, and was nestled on a silk silver cushion, with the shimmering gold flecks on its sides striking a bold contrast. Sebastien explained it was only used during Mardi Gras when he caught her gawking at it. She remembered questioning the extravagance of such a mask.

She rang his doorbell but then noticed the door was slightly ajar. It was highly suspicious and probable cause to enter–to check on his safety. She silently slipped inside and called out his name. A jazz record covered the soft sounds of her footsteps as she made her way down the wide hallway. She avoided the grandeur of the marbled stairwell but held on lightly with her gloved hand to the gold railing as she pondered where to go.

Light from a room at the end of the hall beckoned her forward. She sensed movement inside, and she sped up her steps. She knew her purpose for being here. Tonight, she was determined to uncover the truth and find justice for those who had lost their lives.

Selena cautiously entered the room. It was a large study with an oversized marble fireplace. The large fire crackled and popped cheerfully, making the room swelteringly hot. The high-backed chair behind the desk twitched and caught her attention – someone was in the chair. Her gaze flicked to the window, and she locked eyes with Sebastien in the reflection. His eyes were wide with fear, his mouth gagged, and he urgently shook his head, attempting to warn her. Before she could react, she felt a sharp blow and saw darkness descend.

***

Waking up was a painful experience. Selena's left forearm throbbed with a searing pain as if it had been scorched. Her head throbbed loudly, and her muscles protested every movement after hours of slumping in an uncomfortable position. She garnered her training from the police academy and forced herself to remain calm and assess the situation. She took deep breaths through her nose and squirmed, attempting to grasp the situation.

A thick black cloth covered her eyes, and her mouth was gagged with a heavy rag. She could lift her head, but the rest of her body was bound at the arms, legs, and waist, keeping her seated on the floor.

"Hold still," a familiar voice commanded, though she couldn't quite place it; the muffled sound reached her brain as if she were underwater. "I'm almost done."

The pain in her arm returned, and this time, she heard a buzzing sound, almost immediately drowned out by low chanting. It sounded like French, and she wished she had learned the language at some point. She tried to move but found her left arm was secured in place even more tightly than her right. True to his promise, it stopped after a minute or so. Then something that felt like molten lava was poured over the wound, and she screamed into her gag.

The voice shushed her in what was probably meant to be a mockingly soothing tone. She attempted to curse him loudly, but the gag muffled her furious words as she angrily muttered her rage. Her blindfold was torn away, and she fell silent, staring into the unmistakable face of her partner, Brad Archer.

He gazed down at her with eyes filled with madness and wore a chilling smile. "Selena. Did you know? I've been looking for you all my life." She stared at him in silent horror, even after he removed her gag.

Selena glanced around without taking her eyes off him. Sebastien Mouton lay beaten and bloody on the floor a few yards away from her, but as bad as he looked at that moment, the room caught more of her attention.

They were underground, Selena was sure. The air smelled musty with aged swamp water. A dome rose over them, formed with old stone held together by expert craftsmanship. The room seemed featureless except for the round pedestal at the center before her and the matching circular hole in the ceiling directly above it. Through the opening, she could see the soft edge of the full moon, just beginning to come into view.

"You're too damn smart, Selena." Archer drawled. His accent was different now; the hints of Boston disappeared, and a Cajun lilt hung on his words. "You could have just accepted that La Bauve was behind everything and closed the case, but no, you had to bring the Société into this." He tsked at her in disappointment, assuming she knew what he was talking about. He searched her face for recognition.

A dry, ethereal rasp echoed from the outskirts of the candle's glow. "She doesn't know who you are."

Brad stared at her with that strange mixture of insanity and worry. "That's disappointing. You really don't know who I am, Selena? We have been tied together our entire lives."

She frowned, frustrated and scared. "Archer –" She started dizzily, but he cut her off with a shriek.

"My *name* is Benoît Arceneaux! The first son of the Arceneaux family and true heir to the Taureau Couronné!" His demeanor shifted suddenly back to feigned compassion. He came close and stroked her face with a resemblance to loving fingers. "And you are my last obstacle to restoring my family to our rightful place."

Selena had no idea what he was talking about and glanced at Sebastien as if he had the answers. Though he was beaten and bloody, she watched him squirm occasionally.

She called out weakly. "Sebastien?"

Archer – *Benoît* backhanded her across the face with sudden viciousness, and she toppled onto her side. "Pay attention, Selena. Your family stole everything from me!" He screamed, not offering to get her up.

"Your family brought it on themselves. They were outcasts after they tried to seize control and use our sacred covenant for their own gain." Sebastien's voice was dry and rough, as damaged as the rest of him after the abuse he had taken, but he didn't waiver. "The Breaux family was nearly wiped out because of their greed-"

Benoît shouted. "They died because they deserved it!" Benoît stomped over to Sebastien, kicked him ferociously in the thigh, and stepped on the wound. Selena could only watch, breathless and helpless until Benoît finally stopped. When he turned his attention back to her, his pretentiously caring demeanor had returned.

"My last name is Selena Bellefontaine. My parents–"

"Were Delphine and Nazaire Breaux. They used to rule Taureau Couronné with an iron fist until my father stopped them." He broke into a maniacal scream halfway through, and she could feel the spittle flying from his lips.

"He perverted the magic." Sebastien wheezed.

"He took what was freely offered – the Seigneur Taureau offers to those who crave, and he did. I do. I will have what he sought. I will finish his work and rule this city and world like I was destined to do!" Benoît gestured frantically while he spoke. The name triggered a memory, and she suddenly recalled a fragment of the engraving on the locket. It pressed against her hip in her pocket, but she hesitated to reveal it at this moment.

Benoît looked up, and Selena followed his look. The moon was slowly sliding into view, nearly fully visible through the hole in the cave. She looked back at him when he turned his attention back down to her with a wide smile. "And it's nearly time!"

He stalked towards Sebastien, violence in his every motion. "No! Wait, no!" Selena yelled. "Why! Why are you doing this, Brad?"

"My name is Benoît Arceneaux!" He shrieked, turning back to her and away from Sebastien as she hoped. He stomped forward with deadly intent. "I will take your power for myself. Once I gain powers from the Breaux and Mouton lines, I'll be so strong that I will be unstoppable!" His eyes seemed to devour the light, turning into pits of darkness as he dragged her body onto the altar with what seemed like inhuman strength.

Benoît snuffed out the candle and dissolved into the deepening darkness, simply fading from view before her and drawing the rest of the world in with him. Selena struggled and fought her bindings until she bled, driven by raw animal terror. Her bonds around her waist loosened, overpowered by her desperate struggle. Yet, it felt almost irrelevant as she continued to be crushed beneath the relentless tide of inky blackness, determined to suffocate the moon's light. She struggled against her bondage, acutely aware of the shifting air and the slow, scraping sound of the blade against the altar.

The locket tumbled from her pocket, and she instinctively caught it with a tight grip that made the metal bite into her hand. In response, the light emanating from the locket intensified and alleviated the suffocating attempts of the inky blackness. An unnatural roar nearly deafened her. It spurred her into action, and she rolled sideways, her boots lashing out to thwart the efforts to plunge the dagger into her heart.

The brilliance of the full moon's light cut through the suffocating darkness, and Selena seized the opportunity provided by the slight maneuverability she had gained.

Though he had become intangible, she felt the shifting air around her as Benoît moved. She sensed the frantic, dark aura, searching for the dagger's hilt to make another lethal attempt on her life. Fueled by sheer determination, Selena managed to free one hand. Her fist surged through the air, and with the locket in hand, she pierced the dark resistance, illuminating the abyss.

A disturbing sound rumbled like a deep bass note, and the air grew oppressively thick. Her free arm was being pulled away, but she clung to the locket with all her might when she realized Benoît was trying to snatch it from her grasp.

Selena held on fiercely to the locket with every ounce of her strength, enduring the pain as shards of darkness dug into her palms. A piercing shriek resonated, threatening to shatter her eardrums, yet she clung to the locket relentlessly. Then, an explosive burst of blinding white light erupted between her and the darkness, forcing Selena to shut her eyes against the overwhelming radiance.

As the radiant fog dispersed, carried away by an unseen current, Selena lay on her back, gasping for breath and covered in sweat. Only a sliver of the moon was visible, and gentle moonlight filtered down from above. Despite her unexplainable certainty that Benoît Arceneaux had disappeared, she was still cloaked in unanswered questions.

***

THE SECOND SECRET

Selena awoke with a start. She cradled her throbbing head and wondered what time it was as she automatically reached for her phone on the bedside table. The lamp that shouldn't have been there crashed to the floor, making Selena startle and wince. She groaned and peered through reluctant lashes at the room that was not her bedroom.

Her mind swam in fogginess, and her body throbbed as she flung the sheets off and forced herself to stand. She moved carefully, mindful of the shards of glass on the floor that helped her focus but also brought a myriad of aches and pains. Worried about the unfamiliar surroundings but focused on her safety, she couldn't help but feel a profound sense of gratitude for still being alive.

The tidy, lavish bedroom was distinctly different from her messy apartment. Decorous silk drapes hung over the windows, letting in just enough light to let her know it was day. The four-poster bed she had awoken was adorned with plush pillows and luxurious fabrics cascading from each post.

In the expansive bedroom, an array of coordinated antique furniture graced the space, embellished with petite sculptures, vases brimming with fresh flowers, and, previously, two intricate lamps on each bedside table. Amidst the wreckage of the shattered lamp lay a neatly folded sheet of paper.

Selena carefully retrieved the note, her name elegantly penned on the front. With gentle fingers, she unfolded it. She navigated toward the slivers of light streaming in from the window to peruse the message inside, avoiding the harsh glare of an overhead light that would only exacerbate her throbbing headache. She settled onto the cushioned window seat.

"Selena, I hope you had a restful sleep. Fresh clothes have been laid out for you while yours are being laundered. Feel free to enjoy a shower. Breakfast is prepared downstairs. I will meet you there. Yours, TM"

"TM?" Selena wondered out loud. Sebastien Mouton. It came back to her like a lightning bolt, and suddenly, the events of the night before came flooding back. Selena sank onto the bed, staring at the wall in dumbfounded shock. Her mind raced with questions, and she abruptly rose to her feet. She strode purposefully toward the door, her hand hovering near the doorknob before she hesitated.

A fresh tattoo, swollen and lightly scabbed at the edges, greeted her on her left forearm, and Selena's eyes widened in shock. It was the same crowned goat tattoo that the victims had. Brad Archer's victims.

That was enough to distract her from the shock of

the unwanted tattoo: Archer! Or...Benoît. Benoît Arceneaux was his real name, he said. She had no prior knowledge of him, but he seemed to know about her. However, he must have been irrational. Or he must have mistaken her for someone else. She had only known the man briefly, and he tried to kill her. What motive could he possibly have had? He had been worked up in a frenzy last night before he...

Selena almost reached for the doorknob again, prepared to storm downstairs and confront Sebastien or whoever was down there. She wanted answers to her questions and an explanation for the smoke and mirrors she had witnessed the previous night. She needed to understand what kind of sick game all of this was. However, her attention was drawn to a full-length mirror by the door, and when she saw her reflection, she froze in her tracks.

Her unruly curls cascaded to her shoulders. Her face was streaked with blood and dirt. She assessed her condition, noting the numerous bruises and cuts she couldn't recall getting. Opting to follow the note's advice about showering, she turned away from the mirror.

Selena had to open three doors - an expansive walk-in closet, the hallway, and a smaller closet – before she found the one that led to the bathroom. And she wasn't even out of doors she could have tried.

The bathroom exuded an understated luxury, adorned with antique ceramics and a massive copper bathtub. The shower provided a momentary respite, cleansing away the horrors that clung to her skin, even if the scalding water made her wince as it reopened her scabs. She took advantage of the solitude to gather her thoughts and formulate a plan, although she wasn't entirely sure what she was planning for. Benoît had vanished - into thin air, it seemed. How would she explain that to her boss.

After stepping out of the shower, Selena wrapped herself in a fluffy towel. She searched for the first aid kit, knowing it wouldn't be stored under the sink – the elegant ceramic pedestal sink wouldn't allow for such a mundane placement. Instead, she discovered it nestled within an antique vanity.

She did her best to dress the cuts she found on her wrists, ankles, and waist where she had torn at her bindings the night before. Selena had to stop to take a long breath. Putting ointment on her tattoo was the best she could do. She tried to push aside the unsettling thought of potentially becoming one of the victims she was investigating. Furious and determined, Selena didn't dwell on it for long. She noticed a set of clothes meticulously laid on a bench beside the vanity. They appeared quite ordinary, albeit not the style Selena typically favored. She couldn't help but wonder why Sebastien had prepared such an outfit for her. Her fingers lightly traced the opulent silk blouse, a shimmering light blue garment that felt far more feminine and sophisticated than her usual jeans and t-shirt attire. For a moment, she worried about the possibility of being recognized by someone she knew while dressed like this, but she quickly dismissed the concern. The long sleeves of the blouse would effectively conceal most of her wounds, which were more important to her. After a brief struggle with the zipper, she put on her low-cut boots, which added contrast to her attire. Selena quickly brushed her hair and strode to the door, ready to face whatever awaited her downstairs.

She continued down the hallway she had discovered earlier, entering uncharted territory. As she turned the corner, she encountered a wide, grand staircase made of marble that descended to the ground floor, a conclusion she reached by glimpsing the outside through several windows. Following her nose, the lingering aroma of bacon led her to a dining room. Curiosity piqued, she approached the open double doors and discreetly peered inside.

At the far end of the expansive table, Sebastien Mouton sat amid an array of stainless-steel chafing dishes, which she assumed contained her breakfast. As his eyes caught sight of her, his face lit up with enthusiasm. "Good morning, Selena. Come in." He placed the book he was reading on the table and waited for her with a compact smile. She felt embarrassed but entered the room, her rumbling stomach eager to devour breakfast. She made her way down the ridiculously long dining table to stand beside him. His apology caught her off guard. "Pardon me for not standing up to greet you, but I'm nursing a bruised rib." He explained, exhaling heavily and gesturing toward his chest to indicate his injuries.

Had he not pointed to his wounds, Selena would have had no indication he was hurt. Sebastien appeared impeccably groomed, his exterior betraying almost no signs of the brutality from the previous night. Selena observed him closely, noting the friendly and approachable quality of his features, giving him an unconventional sort of attractiveness. However, upon closer examination, she could discern the marks on his face. He had applied just enough makeup to mask the bruises when seen from a distance, and his tailored suit concealed everything below his chin and wrists. Yet, the evidence was there. A small scab marred his eyebrow, and the swelling from what was likely a significant bruise extended across his cheek and jawline. Last night, she had feared that Benoît might have beaten him to the brink of death. A profound sense of relief washed over her at the sight of him alive and well, yet a pang of guilt swiftly followed as she noticed his empty plate. Despite the agonizing ordeal he must have endured, Sebastien maintained a sense of decorum by patiently waiting for her.

"How are you feeling?" He asked, scrutinizing her face and assessing her body.

She sat in the chair close to him. "I'll live."

He winced as he extended an arm to uncover their breakfast, but Selena stopped him to reveal the delectable assortment of breakfast choices herself. She wanted to dive in but hesitated, fearing she might make an etiquette faux pas. The silence protracted, and Selena's stomach roared audibly in the silence. A smile appeared at the corner of his lips, and Selena remained stoic, pretending not to notice. Serving hands appeared in front of her and piled an assortment of food on both their plates. The silent butler disappeared from the inconspicuous side door. Using her best manners, Selena began both eating and interrogating. "What happened last night?"

It was a broad question, but she wanted to gauge his reaction. His response was minimal. "A great many things. We will be very busy from here on out."

"We?" Scorn tinted Selena's tone, and she mentally kicked herself. He was being hospitable. The least she could do was listen.

He ate every bite of food with practiced decorum. "I hadn't planned to draw you into things just yet, but Benoît made that choice for us."

Selena had a lot of questions but settled on, "What happened to him?" for the time being.

Sebastien put his fork aside and faced her. "He died. You killed him." She choked on her eggs, and shock stiffened her spine, but she kept it at bay, maintaining an impassive posture. Sebastien softened with sympathy she didn't need. "Selena–"

"How? I don't understand why any of this is happening to me." Selena interrupted after she gulped down the eggs. As a police officer sworn to serve and protect, killing someone was not the situation she ever wanted to get caught in. However, nobody and no police were pounding at the door. She continued to assess the situation. "How could I have killed him? He was…" She remembered the inky shadow he had become - no, *disappeared* into. It wasn't possible that he *became* a shadow. She remembered as if it was happening all over again: struggling against the bindings as she fought for her life. Benoît's savage attacks on Sebastien, then her. He tried to stab her in the heart, just like his other victims. The stinging in her left arm brought her back to the present. She rolled up the blouse and uncovered the tattoo.

"Selena, I'm truly sorry." Sebastien averted his eyes. She looked at him, searching for signs he was mocking her and not finding any. "I'm sorry he did those things to you. We tried to protect you from him, but…" He put his palms flat on the table, stopping himself. "Let me start over."

Annoyance seeped into Selena's voice as she interrupted him. "You talk like you know who I am. He did the same thing. You and I met several times, but you know nothing about me." Selena fought against the swirl of emotions that threatened to distract her from getting the answers she needed.

"I do." Sebastien looked at her intently. "You are Selena Breaux, daughter of Delphine and Nazaire Breaux," He started, but she couldn't stop herself from interrupting.

"My last name is Bellefontaine." She contradicted. He nodded, bridging his fingers on the table in front of him.

"It was changed after your parents were killed. The organization wanted to hide you from their killer." Selena had only vague memories of losing her family. She had been four at the time. A young age, even before children's implicit memories begin to form. Though her mother's face had become a blur over the years, Selena could still recall the urgency in her mother's voice, the determination to protect her. Her vague flash of memories wasn't enough to create a cohesive story. She remembered her mother's presence. She remembered her mother telling her to hide in the dark closet and the horrible sounds she heard that night, one she hadn't heard again until the night Vice Principal La Bauve had been murdered. The sounds that occasionally haunt her.

Sebastien was watching her intently when she looked back at him, and he continued. "Benoît's mother took him into hiding out of the city after his father was brought to justice. We didn't know who he was or that he had returned until he revealed his identity last night. I take it you already know about the Société? You tracked us to the school and then came to my house last night." He looked at her expectantly, but she had to disappoint.

"I had a hunch Mr. La Bauve was involved. The commonality between all the victims was the French

Club and that damned crowned goat tattoo-" Sebastien' crass laughter cut her off.

When he finally stopped laughing, he said, "It's not a...' crowned goat.' It's a bull." Selena muttered about it looking like a goat to her, and he went on serious this time. "Then what brought you to my door last night?"

"The person that killed Mr. La Bauve wore your mask," Selena revealed, remembering the invisible man the night of La Bauve's death.

"My mask?" Sebastien asked, perplexed. "Where? It's been missing for a week."

She eyed him suspiciously. "And you didn't think to report it?" She remembered how fond he was of the mask when they first met.

"I was tempted, but there was a rumor the police were battling a serial killer. I didn't think a mask, albeit an expensive one, should take precedence over other people's lives."

She continued to watch him over the rim of the teacup she raised to her lips. "That's very considerate of you." Selena's posture straightened in her chair, and she replaced the cup on its saucer. "Your mask went missing a week ago? That's around the time the murders started."

Sebastien winced as he leaned towards Selena with concern on his face. "And that's why we got suspicious and figured we should try to warn you. Or at least help you make a connection. The problem was, Selena, we knew of you but didn't know who you were until you showed the necklace to Mr. La Bauve.

Selena mouthed an "Oh" as she remembered how baffled she was when Vice Principal La Bauve instructed her to be especially careful. "I thought that was just because I'm a cop."

"I know this is all new to you. But I know nothing about Mr. La Bauve or any other deaths." His tone was genuine.

Selena couldn't resist biting off a piece of bacon. "Why would an invisible man feel the need to wear a mask?" The minute the words left her lips, she realized how weird it sounded to her ears, but it didn't sound bizarre to Sebastien.

Sebastien searched the air. "Perhaps to seem real enough to lure Mr. La Bauve?"

"Yeah, well, maybe." Selena took the opportunity to devour a few more bites of the freshly baked pastries in front of her until she could come up with a better explanation. "The other victims were not lured. They were killed in public areas." A thought came to Selena. "Or maybe he knew Mr. La Bauve would be working late." She started another curious topic. "Why did they kill my parents?"

Sebastien nodded and went back to his story mode. "Power. As Benoît mentioned last night, his father sought power. He, like your parents, was a member of our order. In fact, your family was one of the Société - Taureau Couronné's - founders, as far back as when the Acadians immigrated to Louisiana." He paused as if he expected her to applaud, but Selena was not impressed. She did not have the privilege of growing up in the world of debutantes and lavished luxury. She took another bite of her food. He continued seamlessly. "The ways of our order are...forbidden to reveal to outsiders, but...these are special circumstances."

"How so?" She pressed, having at least the decency to swallow first.

"Even though your lineage is linked to the order, you were considered an outsider because you did not grow up learning the customs. Technically, you know nothing of us. So we couldn't just invite you in. She raised an eyebrow. "Yet..." He gestured to her new tattoo. "You are also one of us. Both by birthright and now by one of our oldest traditions."

Selena stared cautiously at him. "How are you involved in all of this?" She frowned. The impending headache didn't help when she was trying to fit pieces of the story together.

"Our parents were friends. They were heartbroken when your parents died. They told me about you. For decades, they kept the locket safe, hoping it would find its way to you one day. I think they were murdered trying to protect the locket."

"I'm sorry about your parents." He nodded in acknowledgment. "What's the significance of the locket?"

Sebastien paused before he finished. "Once you and the locket are reunited, you hold the power and will be appointed new leader of the Société."

She cocked one ear towards him. "Excuse me?" She paused for him to explain, but instead, he stared at her cautiously.

He raked his fingers through his sleek black hair. Selena took interest in that: for the first time, he seemed positively flustered. "It may not have…You were…" He sighed. "The other members of the Société pursued us – me - to the catacombs last night. They were attempting a rescue once they realized I'd been kidnapped. They were too late, of course: too late to stop Benoît, but not too late to see what you did to him."

She held her breath. "You didn't explain that earlier. What exactly do you think I did to him?" She thought hard, stringing her jumbled memories carefully. She remembered the struggle. She freed an arm and tried to fight him, but he was shrouded in darkness...somehow. She knew for sure Archer was there, but she couldn't see him. There was mainly blackness, but she had felt him there.

The locket!

Selena fumbled in her pockets before remembering she was wearing different clothes. Sebastien tapped his chest, looking just below her neck, and she fingered the locket. She didn't know how she had missed it. The silver locket was around her neck, concealed under her shirt. She pulled the chain to free it and looked at the nearly invisible engraving of the crest, now emblazoned on her arm. Now that he mentioned it, Selena could see the distinctiveness of the bull with horns. It sparkled anew. Sebastien perhaps polished it before he placed it around her neck. She felt a strange connection to the locket. So, rather than take it off, she tucked it back under her shirt.

"That locket is very special," Sebastien began, his voice tinged with reverence. "As much as my parents tried to protect it–it was stolen. I'm glad it found its way to you. It was your mother's, and now it's yours."

Selena nodded, feeling a strange sense of connection to the jewelry. She could feel the metal against her skin, a tangible connection to her mother and a source of power and mystery.

"To answer your question," Sebastien continued, his eyes fixed on the locket, "It was with the power of the locket that you banished Benoît."

The weight of those words settled on Selena's shoulders, and she couldn't help but feel a mix of emotions. Her mother's locket, a family heirloom passed down through generations, had played a crucial role in her recent battle against Benoît.

"I found the locket in an antique store." Having been a detective long enough to come up with a few possible answers to her question, Selena examined the chain for blood. It must've been washed away in the shower if it had been there.

"You didn't find the locket. The locket found you, Selena. It was placed there to beckon its rightful owner. And perfect timing, too, to coincide with Benoît's return. The power of the locket can only be used by women in your family. I don't understand how it works, but you unleashed its power last night and banished Benoît. His stolen powers are yours now, by right. And members of the Société were there to witness-"

"Wait." Selena put an impatient hand on the table. "What do you mean I 'banished' him, and 'power' and whatever?" Her backlog of anger was pushing her forward, but Selena had had enough. "Are you talking about *magic?*" She all but spit the last word. Her disdain was rising, fueling her anger.

"I know it may sound absurd, but soon you'll-" Sebastien tried to appease her anger, but she was beyond that point now and ungraciously surged to her feet. Sebastien painfully stood with her and followed when she stormed towards the door.

"This is absurd! You think I'm going to buy into your hocus pocus nonsense? You've got another thing coming, pal." She stopped just long enough to point an accusing finger at him before continuing her advance on the front door. Selena heard many rumors that fueled tourists' curiosity about New Orleans. She had witnessed some strange things over time, some she blamed on faulty eyes, others as fragments of her imagination but there was nothing she had encountered that she couldn't explain. He might have confirmed it, but she couldn't accept it. Not to say she hadn't thought about it over the years, but it opposed her training as a detective. 'Smoke and mirrors' is what she coined them.

"Selena! Selena, don't leave. You can't run from this – all eyes will be on you now! There's no going back. The magic has changed you-" Selena slammed the front door in his face, stormed back to her apartment, and closed the door to Sebastien's world. She would understand what was happening here, and some bogus cover story wouldn't derail her.

✳✳✳

The media circus was still in full swing outside her apartment. Remembering how different she looked, she purchased oversized sunglasses from a street vendor. With them on, she confidently walked into her building, remaining unnoticed.

Ajan was beside herself when Selena opened the door. Feeding her was Selena's first order of business. She crooned and gave Ajan extra pets as an apology for her lateness. Selena found her phone waiting at the foot of her bed where she had left it last night. A half dozen missed calls from the precinct and another half from the Chief's number. She tossed her phone onto the couch, uninterested in whatever paperwork or bureaucratic bull they wanted from her.

She turned on the TV instead, wanting a break from her thoughts. Instead, the first thing she saw was Archer's face. She found the remote to get some volume and cut into the middle of the story. "...detective Brad Archer was found dead in his apartment this morning after committing suicide. According to reports, in a note left for his fellow officers, he detailed his involvement in a string of recent murders around the greater New Orleans area over the last week. Details have not yet been released, though reports surfaced that Mr. Archer-" Selena turned the TV off.

She noticed the text message that they were waiting for her. She changed into her usual attire and headed out the door. She bulldozed her way through the press and got into the passenger seat of the swat car waiting outside. It was time to go to work.

***

She got a lot of looks on her way to the Chief's office, but she ignored them with stone-faced determination. Evans was in the Chief's office, but the Chief made a shooing gesture, and Evans immediately got up and left, taking a long, almost sympathetic look at her as he squeezed past.

The Chief sat heavily behind his desk and looked up at her momentarily before glancing away. "You heard the news?" His voice was gruff, as if he had been shouting all night. Selena nodded in acknowledgment. The tension in the air was palpable, a clear indication of the commotion her presence had stirred since she had entered the building.

"You're being reinstated. Suits are pushing through that Archer acted alone. Since most of this happened before you were even assigned as his partner, along with the details he included about setting you up to take the fall for the events at Castille Prep...you've already been cleared to return to duty." He pushed her silver badge and firearm across the desk while scrutinizing her.

"You, okay?"

She was about to tell him 'yes' when she heard a small voice behind her, "Say no." She turned in her seat and looked into the face of Detective Aimee Poirier.

The Chief continued speaking, but Selena remained frozen in disbelief. Aimee had been her partner before Archer, but, more importantly, she was dead. Aimee had lost her life during an investigation gone wrong two years ago. "That's impossible," Selena whispered. Poirier stared at her earnestly, searching her face as Selena stared in amazement.

"What's that?" The Chief asked, and Selena turned back in her chair, facing him once again. He looked at her, confused.

Selena shook her head. "Nothing. Go on," she replied, trying to conceal her reaction and keep her emotions from showing on her face. The Chief regarded her with a strange expression but returned to the rant he had been in the midst of, discussing the importance of good police work and the challenges posed by bureaucrats.

Selena tried to pay attention, but Aimee would not be ignored. She came around next to the Chief and started talking over him. "You can't take your job back, Selena. You've got to get out of here while you still can." Her tone was urgent, and Selena remained captivated by the sight of her. She had almost forgotten about the little crease Aimee got on the one side of her face when stressed. Her black hair tumbled from her low ponytail, just like Selena remembered.

"...wrong, Bellefontaine?" Her name got her attention, but her eyes were still transfixed on her dead partner. The Chief followed her gaze to his filing cabinet. It was the only thing he could see beside him.

"No," Selena said, her tone was as relaxed as she could manage.

"Are you sure?" He pressed a bit harder.

She hesitated, but since she had missed what he had been saying, she had no choice but to double down. "Yep."

"It was a long shot anyway." Selena whipped around in her chair again. This time, she was startled to find Detective Thibodeaux standing behind her, apparently having entered the office and joined the conversation at some point. He overlooked her gawping at him, fortunately. He was scribbling notes into a folder in his lap. Right. For a moment, Selena had forgotten that Thibodeaux, despite his many slimy qualities, had been voted union rep for their precinct. It made sense that he had been in the meeting. Thibodeaux said something, but Aimee interrupted again loudly. "You've got to say no, Selena. Tell them not to reinstate you and get the heck outta here!"

Thibodeaux glanced up, waiting for a response. Selena knew she was in a tight spot this time. She hadn't paid any attention to a word he had said, leaving her with no idea of what she should say to prevent them from suspecting that she might have lost her mind. "I quit." Selena mouthed softly. She stood and moved toward the door. Thibodeaux got up to intercept her, and the Chief stood, slamming his chair into the wall.

"Wait a moment, Bellefontaine! As an officer of this station, you need to–" He started his usual belligerent bullying, but she cut him off.

"I quit." She snapped.

"What! Why?" The Chief's face turned crimson.

Selena straightened her posture, refusing to admit that she had now lost her mind and was seeing her dead partner, and if she had lost her mind, she would be no good working in the precinct. Instead, she blurted, "I refuse to work for someone who doesn't have my back," she declared firmly. The Chief pulled back as if smacked in the face. He valued loyalty, and he couldn't deny her point. "I didn't ask for a partner, but you forced me to take him on. Then, when things went wrong, you abandoned me." She emphasized her point with a snap of her fingers. "I don't need that, and I don't need this job to make a difference." She turned, and Thibodeaux was still in the way of the door. "Move." She commanded. He flushed and scrambled aside.

Selena stormed out of the room, briefly pausing at her desk to collect her personal belongings. The intense gazes of her fellow officers bore into her, but she didn't allow their judgment to deter her. Without looking back, she made her way to the exit.

For the next several days, Selena was in constant motion. She broke her lease on her apartment, but her landlord was more than willing to waive the fee (no doubt also sick of the media circling the property day and night). She rented a new place on the outskirts of town. It was a townhouse built in an old salt factory. She claimed the upstairs loft as an apartment, but she had other plans for the open floor plan downstairs.

The move helped the media circus die down, and

after a few days, she didn't see news vans tailing her anymore. However, she was dubbed the 'Black Widow Cop' because her partners ended up dead. She waited with the patience of someone teetering on the edge. Aside from being secluded and perfect for her needs, the apartment was also one of the rare spots in the city where she could avoid encountering spirits.

Apart from Aimee persistently shadowing her and vying for her attention, Selena encountered spirits around every corner. It took her a few embarrassing incidents to notice the distinctive shimmer that enveloped them; otherwise, they appeared just like ordinary people. Selena had to make hasty departures on several occasions when she slipped up and inadvertently conversed with a ghost in front of a store clerk or a tourist, who regarded her with the same bewilderment that she felt.

Maybe Archer had knocked her in her head harder than expected. But after being cleared for an MRI, Selena thought there had to be a single explanation: Sebastien. He casually mentioned magic and mysterious phenomena, and suddenly, Selena was encountering her deceased partner. It couldn't be a mere coincidence. She was convinced he was somehow involved. The challenge, however, was getting closer to him.

She had called and visited unannounced the city office where he worked. Still, the heavily guarded security officials deflected her at every turn once she told them she wasn't a cop anymore. She was getting desperate enough to consider showing up at his house, but she learned from the news that he was connected to Vincent La Bauve, and the media was still circling him.

Since She knew the school was a front for Sebastien's secret Société, Selena was confident that Sebastien had replaced whatever clandestine role La Bauve had filled before his murder. Doubtless, that was why she hadn't been able to get a hold of Sebastien – the whole Société had to be in an uproar after the recent killings, and Sebastien's new duties would be complicated, to say the least.

Either Sebastien deliberately avoided her, or their schedules never seemed to align. She couldn't seem to reach the one person she desperately wanted to talk to, while the one person she didn't want to talk to wouldn't leave her alone.

Everywhere Selena went, Aimee was there. Initially, she followed Selena around persistently, attempting to catch her attention. She nagged, sang, yelled, and even tried to wake Selena from a deep sleep, stopping short of physical contact as if she couldn't. Selena wanted to tune her out, determined to ignore it all. It was utterly impossible, bordering on insanity. Still, when she was about to convince herself that it was all an elaborate trick Sebastien was playing on her, Aimee would do something inexplicable.

There were moments when Selena was trying not to look at her, and Aimee would pull her hair back or snort a laugh at something they saw on the street, and Selena would have a rush of memory. How could Sebastien fake those little personal details? Selena couldn't find an answer no matter how long her mind churned on it, making her irrational.

Selena lay in bed, trying to sleep without success for the fourth time that week. Her thoughts refused to settle. Her insatiable need for answers threatened her to the brink of madness or beyond. She threw off the covers and opened her eyes. Aimee was hovering inches away from her face, staring at her with a determined expression. "You can't ignore me forever." Selena sighed deeply.

Selena noticed Aimee's subtle movement as she sat up. She had gathered from her interactions with ghosts that they didn't appreciate it when living beings passed through them, even though they couldn't physically touch anything. It seemed most had an instinct to step aside to prevent people from walking through them. Selena had unintentionally walked through a ghost on several occasions, and the experience sent shivers down both their spectral and her physical spine. Hence, she understood why they reacted that way.

Selena steeled herself for Aimee's typical singing repertoire and other annoying tactics to elicit a response. However, to her surprise, Aimee remained seated on the seat by the window as Selena got up and tidied her room.

It was a desperate act to clear her mind, as Selena was generally opposed to cleaning. She had always been suspicious of people whose homes were excessively tidy, believing they might be trying to hide something. However, with nothing better to do, she kept her hands busy. After a lengthy pause, she muttered to herself, "What would I even say? Only crazy people talk to ghosts."

Aimee sat up straighter; out of Selena's eye, she saw Aimee's surprised look. "No, crazy people answer themself." She said slowly. Aimee hurried to sit on the edge of the bed. Her fingers gripped the edge without denting the fabric. "I've been thinking about how to convince you you're not crazy, and if I had any ideas, I would have tried them by now." She stood and ran her fingers through her hair in exasperation.

"I could ask you questions only you would know the answers to," Selena muttered, still audible in the early morning silence.

"Like what? How we met?" Aimee got excited.

"Sure." Selena shrugged her shoulder.

"We met at the precinct. You stole my case." Aimee answered.

Selena scoffed. "I did not."

"Yes, you did," Aimee grinned. "You cracked it, too. That's when I realized how good you are."

"I got promoted because of what you told the Chief about me," Selena murmured. "You could've taken the credit, but you told them I solved it."

The silence protracted a bit, nostalgic and sad.

"Yeah, I thought about answering questions like that." Aimee sighed. "But see, if I were just in your head, then I'd know the answers because you do."

Selena thought about that. Aimee was right, of course, but that didn't really help. Selena abandoned her dispassionate attempts at folding. "Then tell me something I don't know." Aimee stared at her, and Selena turned to look directly at her for the first time. "Who killed you?"

Aimee's face fell, but she didn't look away. "I wish I knew."

Selena looked away, turning her back on the apparition.

"Look, I'm telling the truth." Aimee came to stand...float next to her, trying to regain her attention back on her. "I was shot in the back; you know that!" She sighed and tapped her foot impatiently. "I was on to something! I was so close to exposing the source of the corruption in this city. I found threads that led back to city hall and even the precinct."

"The shooter was never found. The Chief said you went off alone, and the perpetrator escaped after he shot you," Selena said, shaking her head slowly.

"That's bogus, and you know it," Aimee responded, standing her ground. "I wouldn't do something as stupid as that! I went into the abandoned house like I was supposed to and had backup. We heard a sound, and when I moved to investigate, Thibodeaux stayed in position, but he was behind me. There was no way someone could have snuck up behind me."

"It seemed convenient that Thibodeaux's body cam footage revealed nothing but a black void and indiscernible noises. He stayed in position; he didn't even hear the shot that killed you," Selena replied, trying not to sound defeated. She had tried for years to get to the bottom of Aimee's murder, but the whole thing was suspicious. Still, there was never any evidence to substantiate her gut feeling, and Aimee's murder remained a mystery. Maybe there wasn't anything mysterious to be found. Possibilities exist that a long-range sniper delivered the deadly shot that coincidentally missed Thibodeaux. Possibilities also exist that Thibodeaux provided the fatal shot. But there was no motive and no evidence. The fatal bullet was not matched to his firearm.

"I wished you hadn't gone without me that day. I would have had your back." Selena signed with remorse.

"I know, but–" The doorbell chimed and ended the conversation abruptly. Selena hugged the wall, alarmed the reporters found her location, but Aimee went right through it. She came back after only a moment, looking bemused. "It's some guy in cosplay with an expensive haircut." Selena thought about ignoring it when it chimed in desperate succession.

Selena paused, then rolled her eyes and walked downstairs to the door. She tossed the door open to reveal Sebastien Mouton with a charming smile on his face. "I heard you were looking for me."

Selena stared at him angrily but resisted the urge to slam the door in his face. "Are you coming in or what?"

When she closed the door behind him, he stood in

front of her, and Selena saw what Aimee meant by cosplay. Sebastien was dressed in all black, complete with a domino mask, which he pushed back on his head, and a short cape flowing behind. It sent shivers down her spine, recalling that Vice Principal La Bauve's killer had dressed similarly. The evidence led Archer to take the fall, but Selena still lacked concrete answers, so she couldn't completely dismiss her doubts.

"Mardi Gras is over." She pointed out. "Aren't you worried about being seen looking like that?" She turned on her heel and led him upstairs to her apartment rather than stand in the dusty, unfinished downstairs.

Sebastien beamed. "It's N'orleans, mon chéri. Anything goes. Besides, no one is going to spot me." He waved dismissively and turned to observe her apartment, which was now more orderly than usual. She wanted to ask what made him so sure, but he spoke first. "I've come to invite you to a ball."

He extended an invitation, a silver envelope with her name elegantly scripted in calligraphy. Selena hesitated, not immediately reaching for it. "What's the occasion?" She folded her arms and locked eyes with him, seeking an explanation.

"It's a masquerade ball, a celebration in your honor," Sebastien explained. Selena maintained her stoic gaze, prompting him to continue, "I should mention that all eyes will be on you. Now that you seem to have fully recovered, they're eager to meet you in person." He raised the envelope again, emphasizing, "They're dying to see what you're capable of."

Selena accepted the envelope but left it untouched on her table. "Why would I want to attend some exclusive party with your secret Société buddies?" she retorted.

"For a chance to observe them too," Sebastien replied, raising an eyebrow in what he probably intended as an enticing manner. While she couldn't deny her curiosity, Selena had more pressing concerns.

"No, thanks," she firmly declined.

Aimee stared into his face, which would have towered over her if she hadn't floated off the ground. "Why not? He's handsome! And he's in a secret Société? What have I missed lately?" Selena glanced at her but didn't respond. She saw Sebastien's eyes narrowed slightly. He caught her glance but didn't follow it. Amiee observed him closer. "He looks familiar."

Sebastien continued, "I'm assuming you're already experiencing the consequences of...your recent transformation," stepping aside as he noticed her growing concern. "I thought you wanted answers. There are multiple reasons why you must attend this party,

Selena." While she wasn't surprised that he knew about her unusual experiences, she was shocked that she might not have to resort to force to extract answers from him.

"What did you do to me?" Her voice was soft, emotionless. Dangerous.

Seeming to sense the danger, Sebastien put his hands up in a gesture of surrender. "I didn't do anything." He hurried on when he saw her eyes narrow. "Really. I know this must all be very unsettling for you, but…supernatural is just a part of life when you grow up in the Société."

Selena gathered herself for a proper rage. "You expect me to believe-"

"No." He sighed. "I expect that you will come to realize it for yourself in time. Unfortunately, we have precious little of that."

"What do you mean?" Sebastien could see that she wouldn't be accepting any vague answers.

When he asked and received silent permission, he sat on the corner of her couch with a long-suffering sigh. Even seated, his tall, lithe body reached a height close to hers.

"Centuries ago, our Société was founded around the power of a local deity. The nature of that deity is…a mystery. Even to us. By design. We call it, 'Seigneur

Taureau'. It gives us certain abilities, and in turn, we follow certain rituals that appeal to it."

Her eyes narrowed suspiciously. "Is killing one of those rituals?"

"No, never." He hastily defended.

"So, appeal to it how?" She questioned.

"Ours is a realm of mystery, shadow, and secrets of the night," Sebastien declared with a sly smile. Selena raised an eyebrow and responded with a smirk of her own.

"Yeah, that fits with what I've noticed," she quipped. Sebastien returned her smirk, and Aimee, on his other side, followed their conversation with keen interest.

He chuckled softly. "Well...yes. But that's not all we do. There are certain responsibilities as well. We have to perform certain...functions in the community. Unseen, of course."

"Like what?"

He gave her a long look, and she knew she had given him the segue he was looking for. "Well, we keep the dead at rest, for one thing." His look was meaningful.

"So, you know I'm seeing ghosts!" Selena exploded. His smile faded, but his expression was just as satisfied. "I knew this had to be your fault. You're playing tricks on me, and I want it to stop." She looked him square in the eye with an intensity to convey her seriousness.

"Really, how am I doing that?" There was a light exasperation in his tone as he studied her face.

Her frustration ticked up, but she didn't let it get the better of her. "I don't know. If I did, I would have put a stop to it myself."

He sighed and leaned back. "I don't know any other way to explain it to you. That's why I wanted you to attend the ball." Aimee leaned forward to watch his expression. Selena tried not to get distracted. "But it's definitely not me." He put his hands up. "It's you. Your new abilities are manifesting." He stared at her uncovered tattoo. Self-consciously, she tucked her arm behind her. It was still too raw for her to get it removed. "Here."

Sebastien held out a hand, indicating her arm. She eyed him skeptically but was willing to indulge him out of curiosity. He supported her forearm in his smooth palm and gently laid his other hand over her tattoo. He closed his eyes for a moment. Selena tried not to get distracted by the citrusy fragrance of his aftershave. When he opened his palm, he offered her arm for inspection.

Selena stared at her arm in astonishment; her tattoo was gone. "It's vanished!" She exclaimed in disbelief, her fingers instinctively tracing the area where the tattoo had once been. The skin still tingled with a faint sting, causing her to pause. However, there was no sign of the tattoo or any covering that could have concealed the tattoo.

"It's still there," Sebastien explained. "Hiding things is one of my specialties. It won't appear again unless you want it to or are in one of our private places."

Selena's words slipped out thoughtlessly. "The victim's tattoos weren't invisible." The silence that followed made her acutely aware of her blunder. To Sebastien, they weren't just 'the victims'; they might have been people he knew, even friends. She hurriedly tried to find a way to amend her tactless statement, but Sebastien spoke before she could formulate a response.

"Your magic is fueling the spell, so the illusion will fade if you die." Selena smoothed a hand over her sore arm, looking for whatever smoke and mirrors made this trick possible.

"How does it work?" She huffed in frustration.

"If you want answers, you must attend the ball tonight." To his credit, he kept the smug smile she could hear in his tone off his face.

"I don't want to come to your party." Selena crossed her arms and uncrossed them, not liking the sulkiness she heard in her voice.

"But if you don't come, you won't be able to investigate further: the Société, the magic, me. You'll be stuck where you've been for the last few days. Am I right?" She frowned.

Aimee laughed, "I like his power of persuasion."

Selena's desire to investigate spurred her forward, but Sebastien had done that deliberately - used her desire to get to the bottom of things to persuade her. She knew it. He knew it. It was colossally irksome. But would she let that stop her? Absolutely not.

"Fine. Where is this party? What do I need to wear?" She looked down at her sweatpants and thought about her one "fancy" dress. It was plain black and far from extravagant. She had bought it for Aimee's funeral. She glanced at Aimee, who was still watching Sebastien. Selena couldn't be sure if it were out of curiosity or admiration.

A pleased smile crept on Sebastien's face as he declared. "I have the perfect outfit for you." Selena was positive she had been seduced by the mischievous flicker in his sapphire blue eyes.

✳✳✳

"Why didn't you tell me this before?" Selena tried to

keep the shards of anger out of her voice with mediocre success.

"You didn't let me finish," Sebastien defended as they were chauffered down the deserted streets.

Selena looked out the window and counted back from ten. The dark-tinted windows on his luxury car made the evening three shades darker. When finished, she said, "So let me get this straight. I am the new leader of your little group because I have the most…power?" She still didn't want to say magic. Selena was starting to rethink her decision. She was driven by a deep sense of curiosity to know the appeal of an organization that would prompt someone to murder. And after Sebastien's illusion with her arm, her curiosity got the better of her.

"Correct," Sebastien nodded. Under his cape, he was dressed in a tailored suit that alluded to his wealth— Selena draped in a deep purple dress that hugged her bodice flawlessly and flared from her waist to her ankles. The silk fabric reflected the luxury of wealth, which Selena was not accustomed to. She couldn't help but wonder how Sebastien always seemed to get her size right without considering her preferred style, or maybe he intentionally ignored it.

He had called to reserve a small squad of stylists who had been waiting for her back at his house, and they had both primped and prepared her for several hours, with only a minimal amount of swearing on her part.

Selena continued, "I have this power because I got all the power Benoît had taken from all his victims."

"Plus, your preexisting power." He finished for her. "As the last member of the Breaux line, that is not insignificant." Not wanting to get lost in the nitpick, Selena pushed on.

"What powers? I don't have any powers." She tried to reason.

"You do," his tone was flat. "You just weren't trained to use it."

"Okay," she heaved. "And if I bail on all this, it would create a power vacuum…"

"And you're needed," Sebastien added reassuringly. "We serve an essential role in the city. We might fall short of our duties without you and your power."

"What happens then?" Selena wanted to know.

He looked out the window with a pained look. "You don't want to know."

"Won't I need to know?" She raised an eyebrow when he looked at her.

He sighed, "I suppose you will." He smiled lightly, "But not all at once. Let's get through tonight first."

The car carried them across the river and into a

nondescript building. A garage door opened silently and lowered behind them as soon as they entered. It appeared pitch dark outside the windows, and Selena consciously surveyed her surroundings to orient herself. She was rethinking her decision, but the car stopped on a vehicle turntable and started to be lowered underground. She was no longer a police officer. Without the security of her firearm, venturing into an unfamiliar place left her with a slight unease.

As the car lowered to a halt, she tried to hastily open her door when Sebastien gestured for her to don her mask. Hers was an eggplant-purple mask that harmonized with her dress, embellished with silver-edged feathers on one side. The excitement of attending a fancy ball quickly waned when she saw they had arrived at another dull parking garage. She followed Sebastien across the lot to an elevator tucked out of sight. He pressed the elevator button, but instead of the elevator doors opening, the concealed doors on the side parted, and Sebastien proceeded through them.

There was a typical coat check area resembling that of a nightclub. It occurred to Selena that this might indeed be a nightclub; she could discern the pulsating music from further within. The coat check attendant also wore a mask, and curious eyes stared through before he hurried away. They ventured in, and Selena's keen alertness blended with nervousness. Sebastien stayed close as they came around the dimly lit corner, putting a hand on the small of her back. She glanced at him, and for the first time, she thought he looked nervous. For some inexplicable reason, that also heightened her nervousness.

Aimee, who had gone ahead when they stopped at coat check, came back through the wall to their right. "Whooo, girl. You would not believe what they are getting up to in there." She fanned herself, and Selena flushed, suddenly unprepared for the unknown.

Deep shadows and distorted lighting consumed them as soon as they entered the ball. The dim light was just enough to navigate without revealing the mysterious edges of the space. As far as Selena could see, there were several rooms, and each room was connected to the others at odd angles – in corners rather than at the end of hallways. The narrow passages curved in a way that obstructed visibility, making it nearly impossible to maintain a straight view across any given area. The disorienting catacomb-like layout made it increasingly challenging to maintain her sense of direction.

Sebastien guided her through each of the chambers, staying close and guiding her between various anonymous groups of strangers. Each room was filled with people wearing masks engaged in activities that were difficult to make out fully in the dark. Some were engaging in lascivious behavior, and Selena quickly averted her gaze, not wanting to stare openly at their activities.

Some of the masked people regarded her closely as she went by. Some outright stared. Selena could feel the masked eyes piercing into her skin. They watched her with more interest than she wanted. She silently questioned how they were able to distinguish her from the group. Before long, she noticed she was the only one wearing purple and silver. Everyone else, including Sebastien, was strictly wearing black.

Sebastien made a few nameless introductions. Selena smirked as he addressed everyone as 'good sir' or 'kind lady' and gestured to Selena. Most only nodded to her with curious eyes before Sebastien encouraged her along to someone else. One individual caught Selena's attention. A silver-haired woman with a stick neck and back to match. Her black dress was adorned with a sash, whose underside peeked out with glimpses of a red fabric when she moved. "Quiet evening, Madame." Sebastien greeted her as much as he had for all the other masked faces they had met.

To Selena's surprise, this one spoke in a tart voice. "Ah, our newest member."

She felt Sebastien's hand stiffen on her arm, and Selena became more attentive. This must not be the usual protocol, but the significance of that eluded Selena. The woman's sharp smile turned towards Selena, and she met it with the most astonishing indifference.

"Have you come to prove yourself to us?" Selena gritted her teeth. *Prove* herself to them? Why? She hadn't asked for any of this. She didn't say any of that out loud, though.

Refusing to let this ostentatious woman gain the upper hand, Selena opened her mouth to refute the demands to prove herself, but Sebastien spoke first. "This is just an informal gathering, Madame." He cut in smoothly. "A symposium for the new era: isn't that what we agreed?" There was a certain edge to the way he said it.

"Come now, dear. You can't expect us not to be curious." Her voice escalated just enough to carry to the nearby ears, slowly turning their attention towards them. Even Aimee, who had been off exploring with a mischievous grin, came over to watch with rapt interest. Madame incited the nearby crowd. "Wouldn't it be *fun* if we could see what our *new leader* is capable of?" Her voice was light and cloying, laced with underlying irritation. Selena deduced she was mad about Selena being named the new leader.

"What did you have in mind?" Selena challenged, raising a pert eyebrow the other woman probably couldn't see. Sebastien put a warning hand on her back, but Selena was not about to back down. There was a short silence, and Madame Red Sash, what Selena dubbed her, looked stunned before a vicious grin twisted the corners of her prudish mouth.

She stepped back and beckoned a masked man who wheeled forward a sizeable, lacquered black box with a silver tassel. Two more boxes, in varying sizes, were wheeled in and deposited at equal distances. A hush reverberated among the assembled crowd and those trickling in from other rooms.

Madame Red Sash proceeded to the center of the room, making sweeping gestures resembling a ringmaster. Selena expected an ostentatious announcement, but the crowd already knew the significance of the boxes. They exchanged whispers, voices too low for Selena to discern their conversation.

Selena waited off to the side, unimpressed. She glanced at Sebastien's location. He nodded his head but stood so far off that she felt somewhat isolated but remained resolute, refusing to be intimidated. Madame Red Sash turned toward her and made a sweeping gesture, indicating the empty area around the evenly spaced containers. Selena folded her arms, prompting Madame Red Sash to let out a light laugh. "Ah, my apologies, I forgot you're not one of us!" Selena fought the urge to roll her eyes. "These are our testing boxes. A person of your power should be able to determine which of these containers is safe." Her smile appeared friendly, but the condescension in her tone was unmistakable. "We use them to train our novices, but if you're as powerful as Sebastien claims, this should be a simple task."

Great. Selena walked forward, studying the boxes and buying time. "So, I should choose the safe box?" She asked. Madame Red Sash nodded in affirmation with a broad smirk. Selena was torn. How is it even possible to know which box was safe?

On the one hand, she wanted to demonstrate to Sebastien that he was mistaken - she possessed no extraordinary power and had no connection to any secret Société. On the other hand, there was a burning desire to prove Madame Red Sash wrong. Either way, someone would be happy. She wrinkled her nose at the prospect of disappointing Sebastien.

Aimee came over to her, giving them an idea that occurred to them simultaneously. She and Selena shared a discreet conspiratorial smile, and Aimee shoved her face through the side of the first box. She pulled it back after a moment, making a face. "Snake." She revealed.

They circled the boxes, repeating the process. The second box was spiders, Aimee had informed her while shuddering. At the third box, Aimee looked shocked. "It's a baby alligator! How'd they even get it in the box!? *Why*, though?" She started muttering about weirdoes, but Selena was busy thinking. They all seemed like dangerous creatures.

As Selena focused on the boxes, her sight sharpened, allowing her to visualize the animals moving inside. She blinked in surprise, wondering if it was due to Aimee's information. But as their colors sharpened in her view, Selena wondered if this was one of her powers.

Most likely, the Brown Recluse Spider that was native to Louisiana. Poisonous but potentially survivable.

Stealing a glance at the ringleader of this little event, Selena guessed that there wasn't necessarily supposed to be one.

The snake was a light brown color with dark brown spots. That described a lot of snakes. Which one was the *safe* box? Selena had a hunch, and seeing no better option, she held eye contact with Madame Red Sash as she lifted the lid off the box and silently prayed.

The snake lifted free of the container with a hiss, and the crowd applauded with demure appreciation. Madame Red Sash's neck stiffened further, and Selena knew she had passed the test.

Sebastien suddenly appeared beside her and guided her away as the attendants returned to retrieve the snake and reclaim the other boxes. As they passed Madame Red Sash on their way out of the room, Selena said smugly, "You will return that alligator where you got it, won't you?" The woman snapped her attention away as Selena strode past her and out of the room.

Sebastien had been thrilled with her performance at the party. Selena wasn't the only one surprised; everyone present had been caught off guard when she passed the test with flying colors. The bullsnake, a significant symbol for the Société, had solidified her new role as their leader, albeit unwanted. Sebastien had delivered this news with the excitement of a child on Christmas morning.

Selena didn't want to lead anyone; she was a loner, plain and simple. That suited her, and she liked only being responsible for herself – and Ajan but that was because she had no family, and Ajan filled that emotional void for her. Yet, there was something in Sebastien's eyes when she said as much - fear. She knew he meant it when he said she was needed. The scope of what her new role would entail was still mostly a mystery to her. Apparently, she wasn't done proving herself.

As they journeyed home from the party, Sebastien couldn't contain his praise for her performance and promptly delved into discussions about her upcoming assignments. As the potential new leader, it seemed that she had until the next new moon to undergo more 'tests.' Each time Sebastien presented her with a new task, Selena reacted to the prospect in novel and increasingly intriguing ways.

A week later, as Selena stood outside the deteriorating cemetery, a crowbar clutched in one hand and a flashlight in the other, couldn't help but feel a pang of uncertainty. With alarming speed, she had transitioned from one side of the law to another. The cemetery's gate stood before her, its rusty bars fused and bolstered by a looming fence that arched toward the street. Cemeteries held a unique significance in the culture and folklore of New Orleans. While most were open to the public, and a few even conducted regular tours to showcase their famous occupants, what Selena was contemplating now was far from ordinary.

This cemetery was tucked away from prying eyes as effectively as possible. Those in the know, including Selena, who used to be a cop, knew this place had a sinister reputation. Several prospective grave robbers and thrill-seekers vanish mysteriously. Such rumors, if they gained traction, had the potential to draw the wrong kind of attention—hordes of people who sought morbid thrills. Consequently, it was imperative to keep this hidden gem under wraps.

Thankfully, at first glance, there was nothing remarkable about the cemetery. The small piece of land appeared ordinary when viewed through the fenced bars. It constituted an open space, primarily visible from any spot along the perimeter. Occasionally, a mausoleum would disrupt the otherwise unassuming landscape.

Sebastien had made an unequivocal promise that this would be the ultimate test, with no further trials to follow. However, he imposed a strict deadline, insisting it had to be completed before the upcoming new moon, which was only a few days away. Upon successfully exiting the cemetery, she would finally receive full recognition as the new leader of the Taureau Couronné Société. It only added to her nervousness when Sebastien cautioned that this trial could potentially be the most dangerous yet.

Despite her persistent inquiries, Sebastien remained tight-lipped about the specifics of the test, divulging no further information. He had, however, emphasized that she must not bring her spectral companion along. He was aware of Aimee's presence but had refrained from delving deeper into the matter.

As Selena stepped onto the soft earth after successfully clearing the fence, she noted the scarce footprints in the area. This cemetery saw few visitors, and the grass grew in uneven patches amidst the rich, loamy soil.

Following Sebastien's instructions, she made her way to the center of the plot. She fingered the key he gave her. It was heavy for its size, cast iron maybe, and very old, she guessed by the intricate design. When Selena reached what she thought was the center of the cemetery plot, she glanced around. There was supposed to be a door, but there was nothing she could see. There were graves – modest headstones with names worn away by time. She examined them, looking for a place to use her key without success.

Frustration crept in, but Selena searched again. She walked to the fence and paced across, counting steps. Using her makeshift measuring system, she found that she had been close to halfway across in her initial guess and planted herself there thinking.

Then she looked down. The grass below her was dry and tangled, and she stood atop a small mound right where the center ought to be. Operating on a hunch, she touched the ground below her. It was cold. Colder than it should be in the warm evening air.

Selena alternated between her fingers and the crowbar, which Sebastien thought would help, to dig away the dirt until she revealed a chiseled round stone below the surface. She used the crowbar to ease it aside to find a metal plate covering. She dusted the loose dirt off her jeans and planted her boots while looking down to inspect the design. A goat – no, a bull! – carved into the metal covering. Selena knew she was in the right place. As she placed one hand for support on the metal plate, it effortlessly glided aside, revealing another metal cover - with a keyhole. As she retrieved the key from the ground beside her, she knew the key would fit even before she inserted it, and as soon as she did, she reflexively yanked her hand away.

The key turned on its own.

The cover hissed and scrolled out of sight, causing her to hastily retract with a shiver as cold air hurriedly escaped from the interior. Selena inhaled a slow breath through her nose, taking a moment to push her down her fear. Her biggest regret was thinking she didn't need more than just the T-shirt she wore. She took a moment to briskly appease the goosebumps that surfaced on her upper arms. Her efforts were futile as a thick fog swept through the fence, enhancing the spookiness of the graveyard. Selena circled, trying not to miss anything - or anyone - that may have been swept in with the fog that threatened to engulf her.

She stood frozen, staring into the obscure interior of the manhole. Her knees locked, and she strongly considered going home. Sebastien said this was only something she could do. She wondered how an orphaned girl was tasked with such a mighty role. It was essential to the safety of all New Orleans, he emphasized. Selena cringed and mentally kicked herself for that moment of gullibility. Yet her curiosity pushed her forward.

The cold that spilled from the hole sank into her bones. It was a chill more overwhelming than the depths of winter, and it threatened her with a feathery brush of a frosty tendril that slid across the ground around her ankles.

Sebastien had told her she would only get one chance to impress "The Gardiennes." They were named such because they refused and consumed all other names that had been presented to them. She wished now she had asked what would happen if she failed to impress, but the answer was obvious, right? Maybe she should have taken Sebastien more seriously.

Selena squeezed her hands into fists and took sharp, deep breaths. She crouched and slipped her fingers into the thin crack of the rounded cover. She attempted to avoid dwelling on those moments in adventure films when a character inserted their arm into a hole, and you couldn't help but anticipate something biting it off.

It was cold, and she used that as motivation and hastily sat on the edge and slid her feet into the bleak and mysterious hole that yawned at her feet. Sebastien also gave her a flashlight, but wary of being seen from the street, she cupped her hand around the beam as she shone the light downward. She wasn't sure what she was searching for or how to recognize it if she saw it. She shone the circle of light on the grass to ensure the flashlight worked, but it vanished when she redirected the beam toward the hole. The darkness consumed her light, leaving no trace.

Hair standing on end, Selena reached a tentative hand into the pit. When nothing reached up and grabbed her, she felt for a ladder or anything at all to help her descent. Her hand only found smooth stone in a circle as deep as she dared reach.

She retracted her hand and was happy it returned to her unbesmirched. She studied her hand, flipping it from one side to the other as if she expected it to reveal something where it had disappeared into the darkness.

Seeing no other option, Selena sat on the edge and stuck her legs in, cringing. Again, nothing happened, but she also couldn't find anything to hold onto. Deeper, she could feel the hole open up into an unknown, more expansive space, but there was still nothing to hold onto and no way to know how deep it was. Should she go back for a rope? Sebastien had said she wouldn't need anything more than what he had gifted her.

Seeing no other option, Selena lowered herself until she was hanging by her fingertips. It was particularly terrifying when her head sunk below the rim.

She had a moment while she dangled, feeling nothing below or around her in any direction, to regret her choices. She couldn't help holding her breath as she frantically decided to pull herself back up. Unfortunately, another decision was made for her. Her grip disappeared, and she was yanked downward into the depths.

Selena vaguely remembered landing hard enough to shock her system. She was disoriented by the dark but felt as if she was sitting up when she regained her senses.

"I thought you were going to dangle all day like a

fish, Sha," said a female voice. The gentle voice reminded her of a grandmother, but the shivers coursing down her spine reminded Selena to be careful. "How brave of you to venture this far.".

Selena blinked, realizing her eyes were open, though nothing reached them. It was an odd feeling not to be able to see, knowing her eyes were wide open. The darkness was like a blanket over her face.

"Ah, Selena, such a lovely name. I remember when your mother came on her quest."

Selena's interest piqued. "You knew my mother?" She warmed with curiosity. The air was so thick she expected her voice to sound muffled, but she sounded normal, casual even, to her ears.

"Of course." The voice confirmed. "Many great leaders have come through me. She came to see me many, many moons ago herself. She jumped right in here." The woman laughed with pride. "I liked that. Knew right then she would make a great Gardienne."

"Um…what's a Gardienne?" Selena asked, turning around. The voice seemed to be everywhere, as the air seemed to shift in different places. She could tell immediately it was the wrong question. The air dropped several degrees, and it became harder to breathe.

"It's not what, it's who. Why are you here, silly girl?"

Scolded the voice.

Selena opened her mouth and stopped. She needed to make sure her answer was a good one. But what would be a good question to get the answer? She decided to be honest. "I'm new. To the Société, I mean. I came because they said I was needed."

"Is that what you do? What you're told?" The voices all but jeered.

"That's not what I meant." Selena kept her tone respectful. "I don't know what all this is about yet, but they said I was needed. To keep people safe. To help the city."

Murmurs permeated the black air in a cacophony of alternating hissing until one spoke. "And who is this 'they' who tells you what is needed?"

Selena hesitated. How would she explain the fanciful, enigmatic Sebastien to a disembodied voice? "Someone I trust."

There was a prolonged silence, and Selena couldn't help but hope that Sebastien would remember to look after Ajan in her absence. As she stood there, feeling the weight of her responsibilities and the mysteries surrounding her, the voice returned, its tone friendly and soothing, as if it were a comforting presence in the air. The chill that had settled around her dissipated, replaced by a gentle warmth that enveloped her.

"It is good to know who to trust," the voice murmured, words carrying a sense of wisdom. "But it is you who will decide what is needed. You have a strong soul. Your heart sees the path, and your soul trusts it. That is good. You will make a good Gardienne des Ames—a protector of the locket."

Selena listened intently; her curiosity piqued even further. The power of the locket was a source of intrigue and wonder, and now, standing at the precipice of understanding, she couldn't resist asking, "What is the power of the locket?"

The air around her seemed to shift, and the pressure in the atmosphere began to mount. It was as if unseen forces were converging upon her, gathering around her like a protective cocoon. Selena's head started to swim; the sensation was almost overwhelming.

"Call on the power of the souls," the voice whispered, its words vibrating with an otherworldly energy that resonated deep within Selena's being.

She felt herself teetering on the brink of something extraordinary, the boundaries of her reality blurring as the power of the locket beckoned to her. Just as her vision faded and consciousness threatened to slip away, she heard one final assurance, "Welcome to the Société."

As the world around her dimmed, Selena couldn't be sure if it was reality or the beginning of a vivid dream. Yet, one thing was certain—her journey as Gardienne des Ames was far from over, and the secrets it held were bound to reshape her destiny in ways she could scarcely imagine.

✳✳✳

The sun broke through the springtime clouds, and Selena caught some glare off the window. Shielding her eyes, Selena took in the new paint job. "Bellefontaine Investigations: Private Eye," it said in large painted letters on the glass. It appeared more pleasant than anticipated, and she smiled with delight.

The new furniture would be delivered as soon as they finished the flooring. Her downstairs made a comfortable office, perfect for her new ventures.

"Looks nice." Aimee appeared beside her. "I didn't take you for the private sector type. What changed your mind?"

Selena glanced around, seeing that the street was mostly clear. "Not sure exactly. It seemed like a natural progression for what I should do with my police and mystic talents.

"You mean after your new old partner turned out to

be a serial killer, drunk with power, and tried to kill you?" There was humor in how she said it, and Selena couldn't help but smile. "That should have turned you off police work."

"It wasn't the only factor," Selena said thoughtfully. "It was also you." Aimee looked at her in surprise. "There is something sick in this city. I'm going to get to the bottom of it."

"Be careful there, girl," Aimee warned serious this time. She shimmered slightly in the sunlight, but Selena didn't need the warning.

"Yeah, I know. But something has to be done." She was pulled towards this for some inexplicable reason. Maybe this is what people meant when they said they had a calling.

"And that someone has to be you?" Aimee asked, laughter returning to her tone.

"Maybe. Maybe not." Selena shrugged. "I don't see anyone else lining up to take on the corruption and supernatural threats plaguing this city."

"Oh, there are people who'd love your, um, *opportunities*," Aimee said politely. Selena snorted, thinking about her former rivals in the police station and the new ones in the Société.

Tethering between both worlds would be tricky, but

Selena shrugged it off. "I'm not worried about it." She said, and it was true. Her life hadn't gotten less dangerous or complicated since she left the force.

"Oh? You're fearless in the face of danger now?" Aimee teased.

"Of course not." Selena shuddered a bit, thinking about the trials she had been through in the last few weeks. "Honestly, it couldn't get any weirder."

Aimee laughed outright. "Oh, cher. I'm going to remind you, you said that."

Selena nodded, "Please do!" I'll have to adjust to this new life.

As they stood there, the memory of her last quest resurfaced. Selena had been chosen as the Gardienne, the guardian of ancient knowledge and defender against the dark forces. It was a role she had never expected but had embraced with a sense of duty.

Selena felt a renewed sense of purpose as she gazed at the sign on the door. She was Bellefontaine Investigations: Private Eye and ready to face whatever challenges lay ahead, both mundane and supernatural.

THE FINAL SECRET

erched at the corner of Selena's desk, the ghostly presence of Aimee Poirier hummed and shimmered in the soft glow of the streetlamps that cast shadows through the office window. Selena remained focused, diligently working through a pile of paperwork accumulated over a demanding day. Their recent cases were successfully wrapped up, and clients were scheduled to return for their final reports in the coming days.

Selena needed to contact former colleagues from her days on the police force to secure crucial material evidence. Her former comrades were surprisingly cooperative, perhaps motivated by their penchant for referring to her as the "Black Widow Cop," a moniker born from the tragic loss of her partners.

Selena ignored the nickname, prioritizing her responsibilities and the need to maintain a professional reputation. The life of a private investigator was often challenging, but Selena embraced it, taking pride in her ability to uncover the truth and bring closure to her clients. As Aimee's spectral form hummed softly, Selena pressed on, knowing that her unique partnership, though unconventional, gave her an edge in navigating the mysteries of the worlds. The world she was born into and the one she was thrust into.

As the lights continued to twinkle beyond the office window, Selena couldn't help but smile. Despite her ghostly partner's challenges and lingering presence, she knew she was exactly where she was meant to be, solving mysteries and facing the unknown with unwavering determination.

Plus, the flexibility gave Selena time to take notes on everything she had been learning about Taureau Couronné, the secret Société she had unexpectedly been thrust into the middle of. Most members grew up in the Société, but Selena hadn't, and catching up on their many secrets and inexplicable customs was a full-time job. Sebastien had proven invaluable in guiding her through the intricacies of the underworld, ensuring she remained well-informed about her duties and obligations.

After her night of discovering the Gardiennes, Sebastien was overjoyed. He questioned her with deep, seethed curiosity. Selena felt compelled to recount the events repeatedly, as if retelling them would help her convince herself that it wasn't just a dream. She mentioned the triple coverings and the thick fog.

Sebastien questioned her further, his sapphire eyes filled with intensity. "Did the Gardiennes speak to you?"

"Yes," Selena replied, recalling the chilling encounter. "And it was scary."

"What did they say?" Sebastien pressed on.

"That my mother also came to them."

He nodded but didn't press her for details. "Did they talk about anything else?" Sebastien inquired eagerly.

Selena hesitated for a moment, trying to recall every detail. "No, I inquired about the locket, and they gave a vague response. It was creepy, but I don't understand how going into the hole proves I'm the new Gardienne."

Sebastien leaned back in his chair, his gaze never leaving her. It took several minutes after he responded for the weight of his words to sink in. "You came out."

She nodded slowly, realizing the significance of her survival in that mysterious encounter. Had she not been the new Gardienne, she would not have made it out of the hole – at least not alive.

Selena couldn't pinpoint when she fully embraced her role as Gardienne des Ames - the guardian of the souls – and the mystical secrets of the locket. However, her insatiable desire to uncover every facet of her parents' mysterious history was a constant motivation source. She continued to doggedly pursue any leads that might shed light on their enigmatic past, eagerly seeking out detailed stories and hidden truths that could further connect her to her destiny as the city's protector. She knew that her last name was changed once he entered the foster care system—a preventative measure agreed upon by Sebastien's parents and the director in charge at the time. Both had one goal for two different reasons. Sebastien's parents wanted to make sure she wasn't found. The director wanted to prevent the haunting story that surrounded her parent's death not to follow her.

As Selena rose from her desk, the office door swung open, accompanied by a gust of breeze that disrupted her meticulously arranged piles of documents. Papers fluttered and danced through the air, and Selena couldn't help but mutter a few choice words under her breath. Quickly, she bent down to retrieve the scattered sheets, her frustration evident in how she hastily stacked them back onto her desk.

With a slight exasperation, she tucked the unruly papers beneath the edge of a nearby file box, ensuring they wouldn't succumb to another unexpected gust of wind. Selena straightened up the room, restored to a semblance of order, ready to greet her incoming guest.

When she stood, two young women were standing across the desk from her, watching her with keen interest. Selena tried only to look half as irritated as she felt. "Can I help you?"

"I'm Fabienne Cyr," said the elegantly dressed young

woman with a warm smile. Beside her stood Lise Orillon, who exuded an entirely different aura. Selena couldn't help but observe their striking differences, like characters from opposite ends of an '80s sitcom.

Lise projected an unmistakable 'don't mess with me' attitude, emanating a sense of toughness that seemed ready to tackle any challenge. She reminded Selena of her younger self. Her attire, complete with combat boots and a black leather jacket, appeared impractical for the humid New Orleans summer, but she wore it with an air of defiance.

On the other hand, Fabienne embodied the essence of a beachside socialite. Her delicate pink sundress, flowing hair, and strappy sandals painted a picture of someone who belonged at an upscale garden party. The contrast between the two women was as stark as it was intriguing, making Selena wonder what had brought them together on this occasion.

Their brown eyes continued to observe Selena with keen interest but said nothing further that prompted her to ask finally. "Is that supposed to mean something to me?"

Lise huffed a quiet laugh before she answered. "We're friends of Sebastien. He instructed us to find you in case of an emergency." Fabienne nodded gracefully, her composure unwavering, as though she had rehearsed this moment meticulously, and it unfolded exactly as expected. Her poised demeanor added a touch of elegance to the situation, making it seem like they were all playing their parts in a well-scripted drama. Selena couldn't help but admire Fabienne's ability to maintain her composure amid what promised to be an intriguing encounter.

Selena settled back into her chair, her curiosity piqued and tinged with a growing skepticism. "Help me with what, exactly?" she inquired, her tone laced with a hint of weariness. She couldn't help but wonder if some imminent crisis prompted this unexpected visit. Her initial intrigue was now waning, replaced by a more pragmatic concern for the nature of their request. "Is there an emergency?" she probed, her professional instincts kicking in as she prepared to assess the situation.

Lise's casual, "Sebastien is missing," got Selena's attention, and she leaped from her chair.

"What do you mean he's missing?" Selena's brows furrowed in concern, her eyes darting back and forth between Fabienne and Lise. The abrupt revelation had captured her full attention, and she was eager to understand the details of this perplexing situation. Her experience as a private investigator had honed her ability to analyze situations quickly, and this unexpected development had her on high alert. "How do you know he's missing?" she pressed, hoping to glean more information that would assist her in unraveling the mystery they presented.

Fabienne tossed her hair over her shoulder. "No one can contact him-" She started to say.

"That's not special though, is it?" Selena sat back in her chair again. "Sebastien will show up when he wants something."

"Maybe that's true for you." Fabienne raised her nose and sniffed haughtily, her demeanor exuding an air of entitlement. "But this is different. Sebastien is always available when the Société needs him."

Selena could feel her patience being tested but remained composed, allowing them to elaborate further. "What does…" Before she could finish her question, Lise interjected, her tone filled with urgency.

"He was supposed to be present for a meeting this morning. He didn't show up. He also missed a presentation at Castille last night," Lise explained, her words carrying a sense of gravity. "Some of us closest to him have been searching for him everywhere, but with no luck so far."

Selena nodded, her skepticism lingering despite the growing concern in the room. "Just because he's playing hooky doesn't necessarily mean..." She let her sentence hang, waiting for them to offer more compelling evidence to support their claim. The man was missing for less than twenty-four hours.

Lise, her frustration mounting, suddenly threw up her hands in exasperation. "Ugh!" She exclaimed, clearly frustrated by Selena's hesitance.

Fabienne interjected, her voice filled with conviction. "You have to understand, Sebastien has a deep sense of responsibility to the Société. He would never fail to show up without a proper explanation." She emphasized the point, underscoring Sebastien's unwavering commitment to the organization.

Selena couldn't argue with that. She knew well enough that Sebastien had a profound sense of loyalty to the Société, making his absence all the more puzzling. Lise continued. "He's not ditching. He's not skipping out. He's missing!"

"And he told us..." Fabienne slid in, smoothing out the tension. "If he ever went missing, we should find and help you."

Selena considered this. "Help me look for him?"

Lise said, "Yes," just as Fabienne said, "Not

necessarily."

"What?!" Lise snapped, rounding on Fabienne. Selena raised a skeptical brow.

Fabienne shrugged defensively, looking away, and said in a smaller voice, "He said if he goes missing, he might not even be like...alive. The last time, he barely made it out alive, thanks to you."

Those words hung in the air for a moment. Selena could now see that whatever was going on was serious to them. "That means we have to find him quickly!" Lise snapped. A hitch in her voice almost broke her tough façade.

"You're right," Selena interjected firmly, stepping in before the anxiety in the room could escalate any further. Selena continued, her tone more measured, "Let's figure this out together. If Sebastien is missing, we need to act swiftly and smartly. Tell me everything you know about his recent activities and any unusual circumstances surrounding his disappearance."

"So you believe us then?" Fabienne sounded relieved.

Selena leaned back in her chair, her expression thoughtful as her detective senses kicked in. "Telling me you're in the Société's doesn't necessarily prove your connection to Sebastien," she remarked, raising an eyebrow at them. Fabienne and Lise exchanged a glance before simultaneously rolling up their sleeves to reveal the distinctive Société tattoo on their forearms. Selena maintained her skepticism. "That only proves you're members of the Société," she pointed out, remembering that people in the Société were at odds with each other.

Fabienne turned to Lise and nodded. "Show her the letter." Lise reached into her pocket and retrieved an envelope, which she carefully placed on Selena's desk. Selena regarded both women with a hint of caution before reaching for the envelope with her full name on the envelope. The high-quality paper stock was thick and untouched as she fingered it. With a letter opener from her desk drawer, Selena carefully sliced open the envelope. Both women leaned forward, their curiosity palpable, but Selena kept the letter hidden from their view as she retrieved the single page neatly folded inside.

Selena,

If you are reading this, then something unfortunate has happened. In this eventuality, I am sending you my best and trusted students and full members in their own right. There are many factions within the Société, not just the families and various positions of power in our ranks. Some corners are darker than others, and Fabienne and Lise can help you navigate these treacherous waters.

I have no way of knowing under what circumstances this

letter might find its way to you, but between the two, their diverse skill sets should help you navigate whatever conditions you face and ensure that you will not face it alone.

I have unshakable faith that you will work towards the best future for everyone. I hope you will grow to trust them as I trust you.

TM

Selena's initial concern and regret flickered briefly before she pushed them aside, replaced by a more focused determination. "Why did Sebastien choose you two?" She posed the question, momentarily allowing it to hang in the air as Fabienne and Lise exchanged glances.

Fabienne seemed genuinely puzzled. "What do you mean?"

Lise, however, was more perceptive. "She means, why did Sebastien specifically send us? No, neither of us is his girlfriend."

"He's our mentor. Inside and outside the organization." Fabienne supplied.

Selena considered their response, drumming her fingers thoughtfully on the desk. She knew there was no foolproof way to confirm the letter's authenticity; the handwriting could have been easily mimicked. Yet, it was a starting point, and she needed to decide how much weight to give it.

"And what did he trust you to do? What kind of help would you be able to offer me?" It might've been an odd question, but Selena didn't know these women. Fabienne opened her mouth to answer but stopped.

Selena noticed the subtle change in Fabienne's demeanor as she glanced around the room as if suddenly remembering something important. Selena was surprised by Fabienne's reaction to the presence of the ghost. Aimee had been sitting beside her for a while now, quietly observing, as had become her custom since she started assisting Selena on cases. The new addition to the room was the ghostly apparition of a young boy who appeared to be no older than twelve. He had wandered in while Lise was speaking, which was unusual because ghosts typically avoided Selena's office. Initially, Selena hadn't thought much of it, but Fabienne's reaction piqued her interest.

Selena's office and upstairs apartment were built into a renovated old salt factory, and Aimee had told her that the place still made her itchy. It wasn't enough to keep them away, but there were generally fewer ghosts than in other places around the old city. Selena had been surprised when the boy had wandered in but kept her reaction to a minimum.

The surprising part was that Fabienne appeared to

notice the ghostly presence in the room. Her gaze swept across the space where the young boy stood, but she couldn't quite see him. As far as Selena knew, she was the only one, even within the Société, who possessed the ability to see ghosts. Sebastien had mentioned that this skill was passed down through her maternal side. The power of a woman's intuition enhances this ability. That's one reason, he explained, why only women were Gardiennes. According to her research, it was also somehow linked to the locket she had inherited from her mother, referred to in ancient texts as the "*Vaisseau de l'âme.*" However, those texts remained frustratingly vague about the locket's true purpose and origins.

"You can sense ghosts?" Selena asked, her question sounding more like a statement.

Fabienne's eyes widened with surprise. "I... Yes? How did you... oh."

Lise nodded slowly, her expression shifting to one of respect as she looked at Selena. "Sebastien mentioned you could see them. There hasn't been a genuine medium in the Société for two generations."

"I can turn darkness into strength," Lise added, flexing her arm with a confident gesture. "And Fabienne can..." Selena didn't fully grasp the meaning behind Lise's statement, but she was preoccupied with something else.

"Just a moment," Selena interjected. Her attention had shifted to the ghost, who seemed unusually interested in their conversation. Selena took a moment to think, observing Fabienne's attempts to interact with the ghost while Lise appeared confused.

Selena didn't want too many ears overhearing their conversation. She decided to cut the conversation short. "Lise, Search the catacombs. Fabienne double-checked his home. I'll check the school and meet back here tomorrow." She pushed them out the door before they could get a word in, locked the door behind them, and flipped the 'open' sign to 'closed.' She took a deep breath before turning back around.

The boy ghost watched her silently from about where he had been standing in the middle of the room. A vague smile tugged the corner of his lip innocently. "Hello."

Aimee left her perch and approached slowly, her gaze shifting between Selena and the boy with a perplexed expression. "Is this your kid?" Aimee asked, a hint of humor in her tone.

Selena chuckled dryly. "Ha ha, very funny."

As Selena watched the boy, a sense of unease settled over her. Something about him bothered her, but she couldn't quite put her finger on it.

The boy's eyes suddenly fixated on Selena's throat, and he furrowed his brows. Selena followed his gaze and spotted a small red dot below her collarbone. She reacted swiftly when Aimee shouted, "Get down!". Selena dove to the ground just as her window shattered, sending a shower of glass shards cascading over her.

Disregarding the glass shards littering the floor, Selena moved urgently, crawling away from the shattered window, which was now just a gaping hole in the wall. Positioned behind her desk, she swiftly located the button that activated the security gate. With a decisive press, the gate descended, effectively sealing the window and the door from potential threats outside.

Aimee reappeared, passing through the wall and crouching beside Selena, who had taken cover under her desk. "They sped away in a van as soon as they fired," Aimee reported, her voice marked with urgency. "They might be gone for now, but who knows if they'll try again." It wasn't the first time Selena had been shot at. Being on the police force, it's almost expected, but as a private investigator, this was unexpected unless one of her case files had a secret that didn't want to be revealed. She would have to reexamine her files. Selena was perplexed by another thought. Perhaps this was associated with Sebastien's disappearance. The boy had moved closer and was bent with his hands on his knees to watch her closely.

"Who are you?" Aimee sounded a bit snappish.

Selena sighed, sure now, after inspecting his face more closely. "What are you doing here, Benoît?"

Aimee stepped back, looking at him more closely now. "Holy crap, you're right. Why are you a kid?!"

He maintained the innocent facade momentarily, locking eyes with Selena before letting out a chortle. His smile stretched into a distorted version of the charming one he had often worn as an adult. "I wasn't sure you'd recognize me," he admitted. "So, how've you been?"

Selena straightened and casually leaned against the table's edge, crossing one leg over the other. "Alive," she responded with a smirk, meeting his gaze with unwavering confidence. "You?"

He clenched his teeth at her mockery. "Oh, you know. Planning my revenge," he replied, his smile no longer charming but filled with bitterness.

"Oh, yeah?" Selena asked, her tone devoid of interest. "How's that going for you?"

"It's about to go a lot better," he replied with a dry tone that seemed out of place in his youthful appearance.

"Why's that?" Selena inquired with feigned curiosity. He approached her slowly and leaned in. Although

Selena thought ghosts couldn't hurt anyone, she leaned out of his reach. She had seen something in his amber-brown eyes the night he tried to kill her. A malice that looked perverse in the face of a child. "You're going to help me get back at the people who betrayed me."

She processed that for a moment. "The people who betrayed you?" Years as a detective kept Selena's tone and expression clear of how shaken she felt. That meant more than one person wanted her dead. Understanding broke her out of her fear, and she leaned forward again. Inches from his ethereal face, she asked, "Who were you working with?"

He smirked. "In good time, Selena."

She leaned back and scoffed. "You want me to help you…?"

"To take down my former accomplices," he interrupted, but she kept talking.

"…and you won't even say who they were?" She let every bit of her contempt and scorn infiltrate her inflection.

"That's about right," he said, still smirking. "If I tell you who they are, you won't go after them as you need to."

"The way you want me to, you mean," she scoffed again.

"That's right," his smirk widened.

"No deal. You tried to kill me when you were alive, and now you want me to help you when you're dead? I'm not going to kill your old enemies for you." She felt her lip curl with contempt.

His smile flickered but didn't fall. "Who said kill?" His tone implied he would prefer an unspeakable fate, something far worse than death. Selena, drawing on her experience on the police force, had a few ideas about what that might entail.

Her smile dropped. "No," she said definitively.

Maniacal anger raged across his face, and he raised his hand as if to strike her, but at the last second remembered he couldn't. "If I were you, I would consider. They also want you dead. Don't you want to stop them before they try again?" He hissed.

Selena shrugged. "I suppose." She could tell her composed façade was chipping away at him. "But not on your terms."

"They are behind every major crime in this city and primed to move. They've tipped their hand by getting your little friend out of the way. They wouldn't do that now if they weren't poised to strike again." His face contorted. "I was supposed to be the catalyst for that change and take my rightful place on top. But *you* ruined all of that."

Selena rubbed her first finger and thumb together, playing the world's tiniest violin just for him. "I ruined the fact that you want to kill me for power? So why aren't you trying to get revenge on me then?" Selena knew the answer, but she had to ask.

He smiled sweetly. "Why would I do that, darling? You're the only one who can see me. *But* that also means you're the only one who can help me get revenge on everyone else. Sacrifices have to be made." Seeing she was unconvinced, he pressed, "What? Don't you trust me? I just saved your life."

If he expected her to buy that, he had another thing coming. *If* he saved her life, he only wanted something from her. But it would be nice to take down the others before they attacked. It would help to know who they were and what they wanted. The silence drew between them, and Selena let him stew. When he started to fidget, Selena leaned in again. "We do this my way. You give me names; I take them down."

After a pause, a sardonic corner of Benoît's mouth tugged upward. "I don't have them." Selena blinked at him, too stunned to roll her eyes. He interrupted before she could say what she was thinking in the rudest way possible. "*But* I can lead you to them. They function as a web, see." He drew a line in the air with his finger, connecting invisible dots. "They hide their identities, even from each other, but they still have to coordinate their efforts. I know where to find a few, and those few will lead us to the others."

Selena sat back, considering, and shared a look with Aimee. "I'll think about it. Come back tomorrow – at a decent hour." Selena flicked her hand, and Benoît vanished.

Aimee snorted. "Bet he didn't know you could do that." She remarked. Selena shrugged. It had been an immense relief and one of the few concrete breakthroughs she made in the old libraries at the organization: finding out how to send ghosts away at will. She had ignored them at first, afraid that if they knew she could see them, they would start following her around in large numbers, which they did until she couldn't function. When she complained to Sebastien, he remarked, 'With great powers comes great responsibilities.'

"What do you think?" Selena was still mulling, but her old partner was much quicker on the draw.

Aimee's brow furrowed. "Selena, I remember something. We were investigating the death of Sebastien's parents, and I found some corruptions…vague connections that seemed too coincidental," she pondered. "I was going to tell you when I had some concrete evidence. It is coincidental that I got lured into that abandoned building the day you were out sick. Could it all be linked in some way?"

Selena had been wondering the same. During her time as a detective, and since she had quit, whispers and uncanny coincidences implied a larger organization. With what they knew now about the Société, Benoît's involvement with a more nefarious underbelly of the secret Société, and Aimee's murder. "There can't be more than one elaborate, underground conspiracy trying to seize control of the city, can there?"

Selena meant it as a joke, but Aimee frowned, considering it seriously. "I was close to finding out who was behind it before I was murdered." She hardly hesitated over those words anymore, soldiering forward like it didn't bother her. "You have all my old notes. Maybe we can compare those to the Société stuff and start making connections there." She stood and floated around, eager to start but unable to turn pages herself.

Selena started the coffee pot and began digging through her files. "This is gonna be a long night."

✳✳✳

Fabienne and Lise arrived early the following day, their expressions showing concern as they observed the recently shattered window. However, Selena had already cleaned up the glass and placed a board over the opening. Selena introduced Fabienne and Lise to Aimee. She brought out the Ouija board so they could talk as needed without asking her to relay messages. Her irritation might have kept them out if they hadn't come bearing oversized cups of coffee.

After an all-nighter of pouring over Aimee's notes, Selena was staggered by the scope of it. Missing persons, scandals swept under the rug, and deals that went through at the last minute, favoring an outcome that had seemed unlikely before an inexplicable tug on the levers of power. Yet, it amounted to nothing. There was no evidence for any of it. Nothing that could be brought before a judge anyway, but by dawn, Selena was convinced. What seemed like too many coincidences were bound to lead to something significant. Selena couldn't ignore the patterns forming around her—the sudden appearance of these new Société members, the unexpected visitation of the boy ghost, and the mysterious disappearance of Sebastien. It all hinted at a deeper, interconnected web of events waiting to be unraveled. She was determined to follow the threads and uncover the truth, even if it meant delving into the darkest corners of the supernatural world she had reluctantly become a part of.

Fabienne and Lise, to her surprise, had found notes on Société activities in Sebastien's office that might give them an idea of where to start. The notes from Sebastien's office were more complex to decipher since Selena was still learning how the Société functioned and the scope of their operations, but that was where Fabienne started to show her worth. Fabienne, apparently, knew everyone. Or, if she didn't know them directly, she knew *of* them. As they made their way through Sebastien's private notes, mostly clerical and administrative, Fabienne's knowledge started to pull the pieces together.

Selena caught them up to speed before Benoît arrived so they wouldn't reveal too much in his presence. When Benoît finally did arrive, he looked perturbed.

The Société, in its decades of presence in the community, had its fingers in every pie. Fabienne helped them fill in possible names to the web of conspiracy. Aimee had only scratched the surface in her investigation. The list comprised people from the Société who had a controlling interest in various areas of government and other areas of authority that oversaw movement and supply chains crucial to the city. The police commissioner was a member of the Société, as were the deputy mayor, and several other strategically placed officials who, under the right circumstances, could have used their power to manipulate events in their favor. Aimee listened with pursed lips as Fabienne essentially mapped the possible participants in the network of conspiracy.

Selena herself took it all in with a sinking feeling. She had never been naïve enough to think that Taureau Couronné was all puppies and rainbows – unwaveringly committed to serving the city and its unseen supernatural needs. Sebastien mentioned the original basis of the organization was pure, but over time, it became eroded by greed and a craving for power. Yet…it was worse than she first envisioned. Coordination on this scale was…"They can't work together on this scale without someone directing them." Selena cut in suddenly, derailing some of the speculations around the table.

"They could be united by a common interest," Aimee considered.

"They are – greed. But some of this is directed, specific." Selena pointed out a few possible kinks in the chain of events: people who had acted against their interest or would've had to stretch their necks out pretty far. "Some of these events don't make sense unless…"

"Unless there was a grander plan," Benoît spoke up for the first time since he had sulked through the door (literally).

"What do you know?" Selena turned to look at him. His smirk was back. Fabienne and Lise looked between each other and Selena, not wanting to interrupt but unable to hear the other half of the conversation.

"I think I know who the leader of the Silent is. Well, one of them anyway." Benoît was trying to intrigue her, but something else caught her attention.

"What's the Silent? Is that what they're called?" Benoît started to answer, but a sharp look between Fabienne and Lise drew Selena's focus back to them, causing Benoît to pout again. "What? You've heard of them?" Selena directed the question toward them this time.

"I've heard rumors," Lise said carefully, turning her eyes to the corner of the room. "They're like…the boogeyman." She supplied drawing looks from Selena and Fabienne, who made a flustered sound and tossed her hair. Lise continued, "It was something parents told you about when you grew up in the Société. Did Sebastien tell you that only women can become Gardiennes?" Selena nodded. "Well, there were some *men* that wanted that power for themselves. They had to go over to the dark side for that to happen. They formed a faction that wanted to appease the evil."

"They wanted to worship the other face of Seigneur Taureau." Fabienne shuddered, and Lise rolled her eyes. "Back when the Société first got going, the consensus was that we should focus on appeasing the lighter side, but some…thought that there was more to be gained from the darker side."

Selena had learned most of that during her studies but couldn't help raising a sardonic brow, "And who cares about who gets murdered, right?"

Fabienne, to Selena's surprise, got defensive. "A lot of people cared! The rest of the Société fought back, and the Silent were driven out!"

"Or went into hiding," Lise muttered to herself as if the others weren't supposed to hear. When Selena and Fabienne looked at her, she went on. "That's how they got the name. The leader of the dark faction said we would never be rid of them in this big final standoff with the rest of the Société. So people started calling them 'The Silent Ones' because they feared they were still hiding among us."

"Plus, the Société seems to have a real flair for the dramatic." Lise laughed, and Fabienne shook her head.

"And you know who's in charge?" Selena turned back to Benoît.

He sulked for a moment but, unable to resist the one living person he could still torture, got over it. "Of course. You know her too, I think." He gestured to the pile of pictures, and Selena picked through them for him, drawing out one she was surprised to recognize.

"Her?!" Serena's blurted in surprise. She recognized the stick neck and haughty jawline. "Madame Red Sash." It was Fabienne's turn to laugh.

"That's what you call her?" She gasped.

"Sebastien didn't introduce us at that party with the mystery boxes. I remember there was red on the bottom of her sash, even though everyone wore black."

Lise hissed, "Typical."

Fabienne rolled her eyes again. "She was insulting you. She emphasized her objections to you becoming the new leader as much as she could get away with." Lise nodded, concurring with Fabienne's assessment of Société's internal politics.

"They don't allow names at those parties, and colors are how you signal hierarchy. Black is to symbolize us as the body of the Société, welcoming you into the fold, or whatever." Lise had a way of seeming almost embarrassed by all the pageantry the Société appeared to revel in. "Purple was to signify you as a new member. Fortunately, purple is used for both, depending on the party, and sometimes they combine those traditions. Red is…"

"Red is as close to purple as she could get away with. It wasn't supposed to be overt. More like a silent protest." Selena verified.

"You showed her, though." Fabienne raised an imaginary glass as she chuckled at the memory of Selena's performance.

"Okay, so I just made that worse then. I'm sure she hates me extra now. I'll worry about that when we get there." She turned back to Benoît. "So she's the leader of The Silent Ones then?" Selena froze, "Wait, I'm confused. I thought only men were a part of The Silent Ones."

"No, women can also be a part of The Silent Ones. They usually support the men that want power." Fabienne clarified.

"Bingo!" Benoît said triumphantly. "She wants the power for my younger brother."

"Benoît, there's two of you?" Selena asked incredulously.

Fabienne and Lise stiffened and fell silent, accidentally giving Benoît the drama he craved. "*She* was a part of *my* plans. I was supposed to weaken the surviving founder's bloodlines, absorbing their power and taking my place as the new leader when the final day of Mardi Gras arrived, and the full moon anointed my power in blood." His expression was wistful, and Selena wished she could smack him.

Selena interrupted. "I thought only the Gardiennes could appoint the leader."

"That's correct, for the light side. The dark side can become the leader by amassing power." Lise explained.

"But then, you and that locket…" Benoît started with a frenzy. "You shouldn't have known the magic the rest of us grew up immersed in! She let you get your hands on the locket! She betrayed me, and now, I will see her pay for it." He was practically foaming at the mouth by the time his rant was over.

"Why would she help you?" Selena asked. She was getting quite practiced at not being phased by his maniacal rages. If only she could also get used to seeing such irrational anger on the face of a child. Or not. Selena looked away.

"A mother would do anything for her little boy." He taunted. His tone was sticky, sweet. She glanced at him sharply, and he grinned, enjoying her surprise.

"She's your *mother*?" Selena asked, repulsed.

"Wait, Benoît is Régine Guidry's son? She's been

with the Société forever!" Fabienne exclaimed, and Lise shushed her as if in the midst of watching a thrilling movie.

"Régine Guidry Arceneaux." Benoît supplied.

"I guess people will do anything for power."

He ignored Selena's snide comment. "She will be our first target." He gestured to some maps they had laid about the tabletop. "These are some of her main facilities." He started before turning back to look at her. "I suppose you're still opposed to killing her outright?"

Selena nodded resolutely. "That's not how we win. That's how we become as evil as they are."

It was Benoît's turn to roll his eyes. "Then you will probably fail, and they will take over once you're dead. What do you plan to do, then? Collect evidence?" He sneered at the last.

Selena bridged her fingers. "Let me worry about that. You show me how they operate."

He sighed affectedly. "Then we should go tonight."

***

There was no way to know which of the many properties they suspected were owned or controlled by The Silent Ones might contain helpful clues, their missing friend, or a swarm of angry Silent members waiting to stop them. So, they started small, with mostly abandoned or neglected properties. Out of sight, out of mind, hopefully.

Benoît had the code that got them into the walled-off warehouse by the docks. Selena made him ride in the back with Fabienne and Aimee while she got shotgun, and Lise drove. Selena scolded him when he started skimming his hand through Fabienne's face, making her shudder, and she had to threaten to send him away to make him stop bothering her.

Aimee went in first and confirmed that the building was empty and free of security cameras. Once inside, they decided to split up, and Lise and Fabienne searched for the office while Selena chose to look around. Benoît, to her chagrin, went with her.

"So why are you a little boy?" She asked, glancing at him to catch his reaction.

He flinched and shot her an angry look. "You should know why." When she stared at him, his lip curled in contempt. "Never mind. Sometimes, I forget just how ignorant you really are."

He was quiet for a long time, and she thought that was all the answer she could get out of him. Maybe Sebastien could tell her when, or if, they found him again. Right now, they had no clear direction on where to look for him, but maybe if they searched the Silent's properties, they would find a lead without calling too much attention to their activities.

"You weren't supposed to have that locket. It was supposed to have been lost decades ago when the Silent warred with the rest of the Société. It can burn away the darker aspects of Seigneur Taureau's magic." He looked at his hands and clenched them into fists. "You burned away all of what I was – all the magic I had gathered, and now I look like this because only a shard of my soul was left behind to linger here in this godforsaken state." He looked at her with the full force of his fury in his eyes. "Just enough of me remains to avenge those who sent me up to fall." He was almost shouting by the end and disappeared when he was done.

Selena looked away from where he had been standing but didn't drop her guard. She would have to do something about him before this was over. There was no way he didn't intend for his revenge to extend to her as well.

She planned to solve the problem of Benoît and the Silent, but it would take some doing, and she wasn't sure it would work as intended. There was something she hoped to find here that would prove her right, one way or another. Selena waited awhile, tracing the outline of the locket beneath her shirt. She wanted to ensure that Benoît was really gone before heading off to test her theory.

***

They could only cover two or three sites each night, which hardly impacted their assessment of the numerous Silent-controlled properties hidden throughout the city. After a few nights of searching, Aimee discovered a hidden room in a warehouse they were investigating by the docks. However, as far as she could tell, she reported that it appeared empty. When they finally figured out how to gain entry, time was limited, and they had to rush their search. Fortunately, the room wasn't large, and the dusty files seemed as old and abandoned as the building itself. They collected what they could and left before the sun rose.

They had to get creative after exploring all their list's abandoned or neglected properties. Fabienne managed to acquire uniforms for Selena and Lise, allowing them to infiltrate the facilities still in use. Everything was going smoothly until someone took a shot at them outside the Southside clerical building.

Lise sensed the shadows shifting, and she shoved Selena to safety with her swift reflexes. A bullet broke the window where they would have been. They wasted no time running, and it wasn't long before Selena understood what Lise meant about turning darkness into strength, as she effortlessly jumped over a wall, carrying Selena with her. She shadows help Lise bear both their weights over the wall. They escaped without catching another glimpse of their would-be assassin and spent the night at Sebastien's empty house for safety. After that, the motley crew had to be more cautious than ever, only going out in pairs and, even then, only to public places. Still, it was a risk. Their plans to covertly find Sebastien were falling apart, and the strain started showing.

✳✳✳

Fabienne twirled the back of her hair. The stress of searching for Sebastien had gotten to her, and she was at her breaking point. "How do we do this? How will we find Sebastien, take them all down, and restore balance to the organization? There's no higher power we can report to; the police can't take down a supernatural secret Société." Selena nodded solemnly despite how absurd those words sounded together.

Selena decided to share an idea that had been rooted in her mind. "I have a plan." Fabienne looked up at her, a ray of hope breaking through her clouded anxiety. Benoît looked at her sharply, and Selena chose her words with care. "We need to get them all in one place."

"Impossible," Benoît scoffed, while the others displayed varying degrees of doubt.

"Not necessarily," Selena pressed on. "We don't need all of them. Just...most of the big ones. Without the head, the body can't survive." Her listeners were captivated by thoughtful curiosity. "Benoît, do you know what we could use for bait?"

"I do," interrupted Aimee. "You." Selena raised a brow. "They want your powers, right? They haven't struck yet because you're making it hard for them to get to you. So, all you have to do is demonstrate a power they won't be able to resist." Selena conveyed the gist of what Aimee had said to Fabienne and Lise. Silence greeted her revelation.

Fabienne perked up, "Like your inaugural party? It's already scheduled, so it won't be suspicious. And everyone will be there. If not for support, at least out of curiosity." The Société had a party for every major occasion.

Selena explained to Aimee. "An inaugural party is when someone masters a new magic or attains a higher level, and they show it off in front of everyone." She turned back to Fabienne and Lise. "That's what they want, right? The Silent are getting ready to move. They want to consume my power, so they kidnapped Sebastien to have me alone." Selena was struck by inspiration. "If we give them the opportunity they've been waiting for, they'll turn out to see it." She was thinking fast, and the details of her plan started falling into place. Lise nodded excitedly. "We have to ensure they know you have some magic they crave. What's the bait to make sure they all show up?"

"Okay," Selena said, contemplating. "We should spread a rumor before the inaugural party that I possess a rare and mysterious power not possessed by anyone."

"Do you?" Fabienne quizzed.

"No, at least I haven't figured out how to use it," Selena replied, recalling what Sebastien told her.

Fabienne was enthusiastic while Lise sighed, appearing as if the world's weight rested on her shoulders. Selena, however, had distinct roles in mind for each of them beyond just the rumors.

***

"Everything is in place; are you sure you want to do this?" Fabienne asked, a bit breathlessly.

Selena nodded. No alternative didn't involve

leaving bodies on the floor. "Go. Do what you need to do. I'll meet you there."

Fabienne hesitated, her excitement palpable. She wanted to know more about the plan beyond the sparse details Selena had provided. However, Selena couldn't risk divulging too much information, not with the possibility of Benoît spying on her. Despite her apparent desire to ask more questions, Fabienne pursed her lips, nodded sharply, and left. Selena locked the door behind her.

"Are you ready? You seem hesitant," Benoît inquired, watching her closely from the corner of the room. He appeared genuinely concerned about her well-being, perhaps because he wanted everything to go according to plan so he could enact whatever scheme he had in mind to derail it. There was a smug glint in his eye.

Selena glanced at the locked door for protection, then back at Benoît. She hid the locket beneath her dress. "Yeah," she said firmly. "I'm ready."

Selena surveyed the party from backstage, concealed behind the curtains of the grand hall. Her guests, primarily the younger generation of Société members, were thoroughly enjoying themselves. Ribbon dancers gracefully hung from the ceiling, their movements casting elongated shadows in the soft glow of colored spotlights. The audience responded with scattered applause and captivated gasps as the dancers executed their mesmerizing routines.

In addition to the illuminated performers, the remainder of the hall remained shrouded in darkness. Eyes concealed behind colorful masks occasionally caught the light, offering fleeting hints of recognition beneath the veil of shadowed anonymity and lively celebration. The majority of masked figures reclined on the expansive, elongated lounges. Their movements in the dimness suggested enough about their activities without revealing the explicit details, and the forgiving cloak of shadows concealed their intimate interactions.

At times, this all felt surreal to Selena. Growing up without the extravagance of performative parties and the dramatic tapestry of history woven into her mundane life, Selena found herself occasionally bewildered. Were it not for the tangible evidence of arcane forces she had personally witnessed, these antics would have seemed utterly pointless to her.

The ostentatious display of luxury and ceremony struck her as decadent and overly theatrical. During the early years she spent navigating the foster system, her life had been marked by an inability to stay in any one home for too long, thanks to the dark rumors that seemed to follow her like an inescapable shadow. She had joined the police force right after high school, driven by a determination to create stability in her life. While rumors of magic and the supernatural had always swirled around New Orleans, she had been firmly grounded in her belief in the tangible and the empirical.

However, her world had been irrevocably altered when Benoît, Sebastien, and their covert war had collided with her life. The legacy she had tried to escape had become an inescapable part of her existence.

On nights like this, when she stood amidst the extravagance of the Société's revelry, Selena could feel her locket burning against her skin. It was a sensation that had grown more familiar over time. The first time it had happened, it shocked her, a night when the locket had ignited with a searing intensity that had banished Benoît.

Now, she could sense the energy within the locket gathering, responding to the growing sense of imminent danger that seemed to permeate the air. It was as if her charges, the mysterious powers of the locket, were attuning themselves to her, preparing to unleash their latent potential in the face of the impending threat when Selena was ready to strike. A daunting feeling settled over Selena, a heavy weight of responsibility pressing upon her shoulders. The stakes were high, and the fate of her and the Société she had become entangled and hung in the balance. Corruption had always been her nemesis, even within the clandestine circles of the Société. However, she wasn't sure who to strike against, so she waited and observed.

Selena was resolute as she stood there, the grandeur of the masquerade swirling around her masked eyes. She refused to back down, to let the shadowy forces of The Silent Ones continue their manipulative games unchecked. Her determination burned bright within her, a fierce resolve to unearth the truth and bring justice, even in the most clandestine corners of the Société.

If only there had been another way to deal with the dangerous force lurking within the Société's shadows. But Selena knew all too well that some people would do anything for more power, and in the face of such evil forces, she had come to believe that eradication was the best course of action.

Selena took a deep breath, her hazel eyes continually scanning the ebb and flow of the party's attendees. The grand hall was a sea of masks and intrigue, with guests occasionally detaching from one group to migrate to another. Mysterious figures blended seamlessly with each other. Each attire was as elaborate and opulent as the other. However, Selena couldn't help but notice some unnerving attention fixated on her. Perhaps it was the significance of her lavish silver dress flowing gracefully to the floor. The silver beaded bodice seemingly reflected any stray glimmer of light in the dimly lit space. It made her stand out like a radiant beacon amidst the shadowy gathering.

As Selena continued to observe, she became more confident that something ominous was brewing amid this masquerade. After watching for a few more minutes, she noticed a peculiar pattern. The mask-wearing guests around her were engaged in lighthearted conversations. Still, these individuals seemed to be playing a more sinister role, lurking and whispering on the periphery - waiting for the right moment to act.

Dispersed in a circular pattern throughout the room, the masked figures blended seamlessly with the lavish décor. They lingered near the bar, their laughter and conversations seemingly innocuous. To an unsuspecting observer, they were unremarkable, just part of the wealthy tapestry of the masquerade. However, Selena possessed a keen eye for detail. She noticed their subtle movements, the way their masked gazes seemed to linger on her, a silent yet palpable presence that sent a shiver down her spine. They may have appeared inoffensive, but Selena's instincts screamed something was amiss. They remained remarkably still, their masked faces and alert posture exuding an air of nonchalance as they surveyed the room with casual glances. Selena couldn't help but feel like a hunted prey.

The masked figures calculatedly shifted their positions as the midnight hour drew nearer. When thirty minutes were left, those at the back of the room began moving closer to the stage, maintaining their evenly spaced arrangement. As the clock ticked to fifteen minutes, they advanced even further, weaving their way past the unsuspecting partygoers, who seemed oblivious to the intricate dance around them.

The enigmatic figures dispersed throughout the area closest to the stage, with a few daring souls venturing to the platform's edge, slowly converging into an unwavering design, all while the rest of the guests remained engrossed in the ongoing entertainment. The tension in the room palpably heightened as the mysterious assembly continued its formation.

Selena could see them more clearly now, watching them from her hidden observation point. Their eagerness was palpable. They were like sharks waiting for chum. She resisted the urge to stroke her locket, which hung warmly against her skin. There were more of them than Benoît had revealed. There were at least another dozen waiting in the audience. It was hard to be sure how many since she lost track of some as they crossed through deeper shadows.

Benoît's betrayal was expected, but facing the bared jaws of his trap made Selena's chest clench with cold fear. It was too late to back out now, she reminded herself. There was nowhere they wouldn't chase her; she would never get a better chance to take them all out.

Selena locked eyes with Fabienne across the stage, who nodded. Selena inclined her head just enough to show she had seen, and Fabienne disappeared. She would have to trust that they would care for the rest while she turned her attention to the daunting task.

Selena checked her clock. Five minutes until her show of 'powers.' They were getting ready, too, slowly tightening their formation and drifting closer to the stage.

The music lowered. The spotlight on her had been carefully directed to illuminate the stage without blinding her to the audience. She needed to be able to see what would come next.

As she stepped forward to take center stage, they matched her, stepping up and forming a tight half-circle around her. "A present!" One of them called, and Selena could feel magic beginning to surge.

It was sooner than she had expected. She couldn't tell if everyone else had yet to leave the room. "Fabe!?" Selena called. There was a commotion on the edges of what Selena could see, and Selena thought fast. She pressed a hand to her chest, where she could feel their magic chipping away at her, just like the night Benoît had tried to kill her. Her soul felt like it was being sucked through a straw, drawn out of her body.

Selena waited as long as she could before again raising a heavy hand to her chest. She retrieved her locket, burning hot to the touch, and held the silver to her lips. *"Vers le haut, Seigneur Taureau."* She whispered, reciting the inscription with cold lips. The locket exploded with light, and she thrust it away from her face – towards the masked figures that gathered to steal her life and magic, as they had stolen so many others. Hollow, mournful screams split the air. She turned her face away and squeezed her eyes shut against the blinding light. As the light began to subside, an ancient, haunting melody echoed through the surroundings, originating from an unseen source. The shadows of otherworldly beings danced at the periphery, their intentions as enigmatic as the locket's power. They screamed and writhed in agony.

The cacophony stopped as suddenly as it started,

and Selena fell to her knees. Vertigo threatened to topple her with spots in her vision and roaring in her ears. She fought it, unwilling to lose consciousness when enemies surrounded her. When the quaking stopped, Selena opened one eye and looked around. The hooded figures were sprawled, flat on their backs away from her, as if flattened by a wave. Not one of them moved. Lise was hopping over each of them, checking their vitals and putting handcuffs on the unconscious bodies. In the middle of the pile, Selena saw Régine Guidry Arceneaux, looking less dignified than she had ever seen, slack-jawed and drooling. Her usually coiffed hair tussled. There were other faces she recognized as well, if only vaguely. The finished headcount of betrayers would be a savage blow unto itself; Selena's stomach felt heavy.

Fabienne was at her side, and Selena finally noticed. Propping her up and preventing her from falling. "Did you get everyone else out?" Fabienne nodded and smiled.

"We did. And we found one extra."

Lise carefully administered sips of water, nursing Sebastien back to health while Fabienne worked to prop him up. Selena had sensed Sebastien in a concealed chamber beneath the ballroom, where he had been imprisoned, chained, and left to suffer from severe dehydration. The Silent had relocated him there in anticipation of Selena's inaugural party, presumably with sinister intentions after they were done with her.

Selena knelt beside Sebastien, holding his weak hand, which clung to hers as if it were his sole lifeline to the world. His voice, raw and parched from his ordeal, was barely audible, and Selena leaned in closer to catch his words. "Did... did we win?" Even in his weakened state, Sebastien's attempt at humor elicited Selena's weak smile.

The room remained tense as they all awaited Selena's response, hoping for a glimmer of hope amid their harrowing ordeal. "Don't try to be funny. You rarely succeed." His laugh was a wheeze. Selena nodded, covering her slight smile, and brushed his hair back from his brow. "Yeah, we won."

"It was amazing." Lise sounded excited as she continually administered water and monitored Sebastien's pulse. "I got everyone else out the back while they were focused on Selena. I've never seen anything like it." Selena looked at her sharply, but she was focused on Sebastien. Selena would have to remember to scold her some other time for sticking around when it was too dangerous.

"How did you do that?" Fabienne was looking at Selena with wide, watery eyes. "I thought you were going to kill them with...what was that?"

"Souls," Selena said, looking back at Sebastien.

"Souls," Fabienne frowned, trying to make sense of everything they had witnessed. "Souls can't do that...they can't interact with anything real."

"The locket?" Sebastien asked weakly. Lise pressed a cup of water to his lips.

"Yes. *Vaisseau de l'âme*." Selena said. "A vessel for souls. I saw your notes about it. I figured you must have been trying to help me unlock my powers." She inclined her head towards Sebastien. Selena tried not to dwell on the memory with the Gardiennes. They said to 'call on the souls.'

Sebastien managed a fragile smile through his cracked lips as he listened to Selena's explanation. "I never knew how the locket worked. I knew you would figure it out, though..." His voice trailed off, weakened by his ordeal.

Still grappling with the surreal revelations, Fabienne sank heavily into a nearby chair. She struggled to make sense of the astonishing tale. "So... those were ghosts you... what? Collected and just threw at the bad guys?"

Selena let out a weary sigh. She was physically and emotionally drained and had not anticipated delving into the intricacies of her abilities at this moment. However, seeing Sebastien awake and engaged and realizing that Fabienne wouldn't let the matter rest, she settled in to recount the entire story.

"I asked them. The ghosts," she clarified before Fabienne could interject. A flicker of pride glimmered in Sebastien's eyes, but it was likely just a mirage caused by his extreme dehydration. "I thought about it logically. A clandestine organization with a conspiracy of this magnitude must have left a trail of victims in its wake. Most of The ghosts, at least, were more than willing to help."

She wrapped a hand around the locket, which was warm to the touch and seemed unassumingly inoffensive. She locked eyes with Sebastien, who was watching her sadly. "Benoît?"

Selena replied in a soft, confidential tone. "Yes, it was the only way I could be sure he'd be gone for good this time," Sebastien responded with a feeble yet heartfelt squeeze of her hand, and she reciprocated, acknowledging his silent support.

Lise, who had overheard the exchange, couldn't contain her curiosity. "Wait, what?" She spoke in a calm voice. "So, you knew that was going to happen?" Her shock was evident in her expression. "Aimee only told us you had a plan you couldn't risk Benoît finding out about." Sebastien furrowed his brow in confusion, and Selena sensed he must be wondering how Aimee had communicated with them.

Rarely in a position to smugly tell Sebastien things he didn't already know, Selena said, "Ouija board." His expression cleared, and he nodded his understanding.

"Not exactly." Selena pushed on, turning back to Lise's question. She welcomed the distraction from her thoughts. "I knew the souls would be able to do...something." She looked at Sebastien again. "Your notes said it would nullify Taureau Couronné's dark powers."

Sebastien closed his eyes. "An educated guess..." He trailed off with a rasp, and Selena tipped the cup to his lips for another sip.

"They are made of the same energy that fuels our magic." Selena finished for him. "I figured they...with that many of them, they would be able to reverse the flow and..." Selena was reaching to explain what she had guessed might happen and what she had perceived when she called on the locket.

"Banish members of the Silent?" Fabienne asked.

"More like burn out their corrupt magic." Selena sighed. "With any luck, none of them will ever be able to use magic again."

"So you blew the fuse?" Fabienne had a wide-eyed expression of disbelief and comprehension warring on her face. It was a rhetorical question, so Selena didn't answer.

"Do you think their powers are gone for good?" Lise asked, slowly cleaning Sebastien's myriad of cuts and scrapes.

"Hopefully," Selena said after a long pause. All eyes were on her, but she had to be honest. "At least until we can separate them from where they can do any more harm."

"It doesn't matter either way. You ripped their masks away, and the rest of the Société will ensure they are never in positions of power again." Sebastien assured her in a thin, dry voice.

Selena felt surprisingly assured. She had been partly worried it would be impossible to neutralize those in the Silent without killing them or putting more people at risk. Sebastien's silent nod and assured expression took that weight off her shoulders since he knew she would be worried about that.

Lise frowned, trying to grasp the complexities of the situation. "So, what about the ghosts? What did they do exactly?" she asked, her curiosity piqued.

Selena leaned in and began to explain, her voice

steady and patient. "Ghosts aren't souls, exactly. They're more like remnants of a person's will and unfinished desires. This energy strongly connects to Seigneur Taureau and the magic we derive from him. From what I gathered while researching the locket, I suspected it could harness that energy and focus it on a specific purpose. The locket essentially chooses someone to become the guardian of this energy."

Sebastien leaned forward slightly, his expression earnest. "Your mother was a powerful medium, Selena. The locket was a vessel for her abilities, and now it's become a vessel for yours."

A sense of connection to her mother, whom she had never truly known, washed over Selena. She had inherited the locket and a legacy of strength and magic. It was a responsibility she was slowly coming to terms with. "I wish I had the chance to know her," Selena admitted, her voice filled with longing and regret.

Sebastien gently rubbed his hand on hers. "I think she would be proud of the woman you've become, Selena. You're carrying on her legacy."

The sincerity in his words touched her deeply, and she offered him a grateful smile. A silent understanding passed between them—a bond forged in the crucible of their shared experiences and the mysteries they continued to unravel together.

Lise nodded slowly, still processing the information. "Okay... So you had to convince all those ghosts to follow your plan?" She scratched her head, trying to make sense of it.

Selena shook her head. "No, I didn't need their agreement. I just wanted them to volunteer since doing so would burn away the last remaining remnants of them. Those ghosts are all gone now." There was a hint of sadness in her voice as she spoke of the spirits' sacrifice - Aimee was one of them.

"What happened to them? The ghosts?" Fabienne took a heavy seat nearby. Selena's gut clenched; she was afraid of the answer, so she again turned to Sebastien.

He took a sip ahead of time before he spoke. "They go on to whatever's next."

"So...Heaven? Hell?" Fabienne asked quietly.

Sebastien nodded. "I never cared much about that part. What happens next...there's no way to be sure other than to see for yourself." Words about a better place for Aimee might have comforted someone other than Selena. Just now, there probably wasn't anything that would make saying goodbye to her friend a second time less painful. "Ghosts are just remnants of the person, left behind to carry their final will in this world. You helped them release that burden."

Most ghosts had been willing to help once she explained her plan to take down the people responsible for their deaths. Selena hoped that justice would bring them peace in some way. Benoît's unexpected defeat still resonated with Selena. She couldn't deny that the thought of his betrayal had haunted her, yet she had managed to outmaneuver him before he could carry out his sinister plan. Sensing the turmoil in her thoughts, Sebastien spoke softly, breaking the silence over the room.

As if reading her thoughts, Sebastien said, "He would have done the same to you. He tried already."

Selena nodded in acknowledgment. She knew the truth of Sebastien's words. Benoît had been willing to betray her, just as he had betrayed many others. But despite that knowledge, the lingering shadow of his treachery weighed heavily on her soul.

Another person weighed on her mind as well— Aimee. Selena couldn't help but think about her dear friend. When Selena had warned Aimee to stay away on this fateful night and had revealed her dangerous plan at the last minute, Aimee had insisted on taking part. They realized members of The Silent Ones had conspired to kill Sebastien's parents to obtain the locket, and they wanted to prevent Aimee from uncovering the truth. So Aimee wanted to join Selena in exacting vengeance on those who had taken her life. Selena had offered that same choice to other ghosts, and by that logic, she couldn't refuse Aimee's request, even though it shattered her heart once more.

Selena looked away as the room fell into a heavy silence, her gaze drifting to a distant corner. A heavy silence enveloped them, leaving the weight of their actions and sacrifices lingering in the air, an unspoken truth that hung over their heads.

∗∗∗

Selena left flowers on Aimee's grave, a quiet tribute to her fallen friend. The cemetery appeared old and untended, nestled in a forgotten corner where the memories of the departed were slowly fading away. She had mourned Aimee once before, when the headstone was new, and yet the pain felt fresh, as if time had not dulled the ache of loss. Refusing to shed tears, she stood there, silently staring at the ground.

Selena had made a solemn promise to her dearly departed friend the last time she stood there. She had vowed to find Aimee's killer and ensure justice was served. She had fulfilled those promises. There were no new promises to make, yet no solace to find in the quiet stillness of the graveyard.

Selena sighed heavily, her frustration and grief forming a persistent headache that had lingered for days. A familiar voice broke through her thoughts, teasing and gentle.

"Ghosts bothering you?" Sebastien asked as he walked up beside her. "I wouldn't think you could stand it here."

Selena turned to him, her eyes meeting his with surprise and warmth. "There aren't a lot of ghosts in a cemetery. Only living people have unfinished business here." She paused, searching his gaze. "What are you doing here?"

"I have something new for you," Sebastien replied, a gentle smile on his lips. "Something you might be interested in."

Selena's curiosity piqued, and she couldn't help but smile. "Oh, yeah? Can't it wait?"

"It can, if you want it to," Sebastien answered, his tone sympathetic. "But I figured I knew you better than that. How about a new case? You must be getting agitated going this long without one."

Selena couldn't help but fidget with impatience, and Sebastien's smile widened at her familiar restlessness. "Is it a good one?"

"Very."

"Tell me the details, and I'll let you buy me coffee."

As they walked away from the quiet solitude of the cemetery, their hands brushed against each other. Amid the challenges and mysteries of their latest case, there was an undeniable pull between them, a budding romance that hinted at a future beyond the shadows of the past.

ACKNOWLEDGMENTS

I extend my heartfelt gratitude to my daughter, Samantha, whose creative insights and invaluable advice have been instrumental in the creation of my books. Her unwavering support and imaginative contributions have enriched my work in countless ways. Thank you, Samantha, for being a constant source of inspiration and encouragement on this literary journey.

I want to express my deep appreciation to my son, Brandon, whose infectious humor provided much-needed levity during the long days spent behind the computer. Your witty interjections and laughter were the bright spots that kept me motivated and inspired throughout this writing process. Thank you, Brandon, for being my source of joy and comic relief.

A heartfelt thank you to my readers who share the same passion for reading as I do for writing. Your enthusiasm and support have been the driving force behind my creative journey. Without you, my words would remain unheard, and my stories would remain untold. It is your love for literature that fuels my own love for storytelling. I am deeply grateful for every one of you.

With love and gratitude,

Bobby Brown

Bobby Brown

The Eclectic Explorer

Bobby Brown is a prolific writer and storyteller known for her vivid imagination and passion for crafting tales that transport readers to new and exciting worlds. With a unique voice and an unrelenting dedication to the art of storytelling, Bobby's work continues to captivate audiences around the globe.

Bobby is an author, entrepreneur, environmentalist, and self-proclaimed beach addict. With a zest for life and a heart full of wanderlust, Bobby's journey is a testament to the beauty of embracing diverse passions and experiences.

Check out more books by Bobby Brown.

Horrific World: Book I

"Horrific World: Book I" invites readers to delve into a spine-tingling collection of short stories that explore the heart-pounding mysteries and hair-raising encounters challenging the boundaries between reality and the supernatural. The journey takes you from the enigmatic heartlands of Africa to the historical tales of England and the ancient mysteries of Japan. Each story unveils the darkness that lurks beneath the surface of seemingly ordinary places, delving into the chilling myths and mysteries that have captured the imaginations of people worldwide.

From ancient folklore to modern-day tales, these stories offer a haunting glimpse into the collective fears and superstitions that have haunted humanity for generations. Prepare to be thrilled, scared, and captivated by the eerie tales that await within the pages of "Horrific World: Book I."

Horrific World: II

In "Horrific World: Book II," readers are taken on a deeper exploration of the shadowy realm of urban legends, unearthing chilling tales from a diverse array of countries and cultures. These stories traverse the globe to explore the eerie legends that have captured the collective imagination of people from all walks of life. From the war-torn landscapes of Afghanistan to the ancient ruins of Greece and onto the vibrant streets of Morocco, this book invites you to brace yourself for a hair-raising journey through the darkest corners of human folklore. "Horrific World: Book II" continues to unravel the mysteries that have haunted the world for decades.

As you embark on this spine-tingling journey, prepare to be immersed in the chilling stories that bridge the gap between reality and the mystical. "Horrific World: Book II" invites you to witness the enduring power of urban legends and the uncanny stories that have haunted the human psyche throughout time.

_____

Horrific World: Book III

"Horrific World: Book III." The chilling odyssey continues in this spine-tingling collection of short stories that navigate the shadowy realm of urban legends. This gripping anthology spans the globe, from revisiting the heartland of America to exploring the chilling depths of Sweden. Building upon the hair-raising journeys of

Books I and II, this collection now explores the mysteries and terrors woven into the very fabric of diverse cultures and regions.

With Book III, the exploration adds more intriguing locations to the repertoire. In each tale, the darkness lurking beneath seemingly ordinary locales is unearthed, diving headfirst into the unsettling myths and mysteries that have captured the imaginations of people worldwide.

Prepare for an even more thrilling, heart-pounding journey as "Horrific World: Book III" beckons readers to explore the enigmatic stories that linger in the darkest corners of the world, now with an expanded roster of countries and legends.

Natural Tea Remedies

Natural Tea Remedies" provides a holistic approach to medicinal teas that address a wide range of issues, including weight loss, depression, immunity enhancement, promoting hair growth, and more. Discover the power of nature's healing herbs and plants through the art of tea-making and embark on a journey toward improved well-being and vitality. This comprehensive guide will empower you to harness the therapeutic potential of herbal teas for a healthier, more balanced life.

Secrets in Silver

Detective Selena Bellefontaine is known for her

unmatched ability to crack any case, but her skills are put to the ultimate test when a serial killer emerges during the early days of Mardi Gras. To make matters more challenging, she's paired with a new partner, the hotshot detective Brad Archer, who's been assigned to assist her in solving this deadly mystery.

As Selena delves deeper into the investigation, she encounters shadowy organizations and uncertain allies, turning every step into a treacherous journey filled with danger. Unexplainable events begin to unfold, leading Selena to unsettling revelations about her past and pushing her to the limits as she faces the inexplicable.

Survival becomes a race against time as Selena must unravel a complex web of conspiracies and secret histories. Can she solve the case before more lives are lost, or will the mysteries surrounding her become her undoing?